Meet Me at the Museum

www.**penguin**.co.uk

Meet Me at the Museum

Anne Youngson

Doubleday

LONDON · TORONTO · SYDNEY · AUCKLAND · JOHANNESBURG

TRANSWORLD PUBLISHERS
61–63 Uxbridge Road, London W5 5SA
www.penguin.co.uk

Transworld is part of the Penguin Random House group of companies
whose addresses can be found at global.penguinrandomhouse.com

First published in Great Britain in 2018 by Doubleday
an imprint of Transworld Publishers

A CIP catalogue record for this book
is available from the British Library.

ISBNs 9780857525512 (hb)
9780857525529 (tpb)

Typeset in 12/15pt Adobe Garamond by Falcon Oast Graphic Art Ltd.
Printed and bound by Clays Ltd, Bungay, Suffolk

Penguin Random House is committed to a sustainable
future for our business, our readers and our planet. This book
is made from Forest Stewardship Council® certified paper.

1 3 5 7 9 10 8 6 4 2

For Frank, Cormac and Holly,
my dear young people

Some day I will go to Aarhus
To see his peat-brown head,
The mild pods of his eye-lids,
His pointed skin cap.

from 'The Tollund Man' by
Seamus Heaney

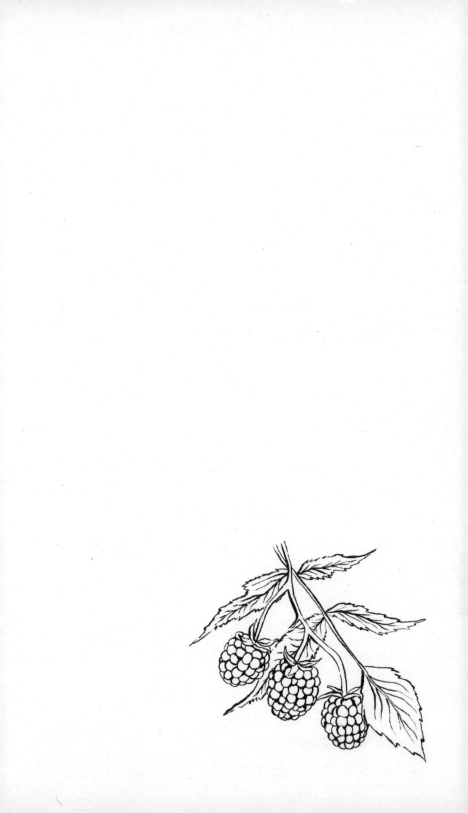

An extract from the Foreword to *The Bog People* by P. V. Glob (Faber & Faber, 1969): Professor Glob responds to a group of schoolgirls who have been in touch with him about recent archaeological discoveries. His book *The Bog People* is dedicated to the schoolgirls who first wrote to him.

Dear young girls,
Home again from the deserts and oases of the Sheikdoms I find your enthusiastic letters on my desk. They have aroused in me the wish to tell you and many others who take an interest in our ancestors about these strange discoveries in Danish bogs. So I have written a 'long letter' in the following pages for you, for my daughter Elsebeth, who is your age, and for all who wish to learn more about ancient times than they can gather from the learned treatises that exist on the subject. But I have all too little time, and it has taken me a long while to finish my letter. However, here it is. You have all grown older since and so perhaps are now all the better able to understand what I have written about these bog people of 2,000 years ago.

Yours sincerely,
P. V. Glob (Professor)
August 13th, 1964

Dear Professor Glob,

Although we have never met, you dedicated a book to me once; to me, thirteen of my schoolmates, and your daughter. This was more than fifty years ago, when I was young. And now I am not. This business, of being no longer young, is occupying much of my mind these days and I am writing to you to see if you can help me make sense of some of the thoughts that occur to me. Or maybe I am hoping that just writing will make sense of them, because I have little expectation that you will reply. For all I know, you may be dead.

One of these thoughts is about plans never fulfilled. You know what I mean – if you are still alive you must be a very old man by now and it must have occurred to you that what you thought would happen, when you were young, never did. For example, you might have promised yourself you would try a sport or a hobby or an art or a craft. And now you find you have lost the physical dexterity or stamina to take it up. There will be reasons why you never did but none of them is good enough. None of them is the clincher. You cannot say: I planned to take up oil painting but I couldn't because I turned out to be allergic to a chemical in the paint. It is just that life goes on from day to day and that

1

one moment never arrives. In my case, I promised myself I would travel to Denmark and visit the Tollund Man. And I have not. I know, from the book you dedicated to me, that only his head is preserved, not his beautiful hands and feet. But his face is enough. His face, as it appears on the cover of your book, is pinned up on my wall, I see it every day. Every day I am reminded of his serenity, his dignity, his look of wisdom and resignation. It is like the face of my grandmother, who was dear to me. I still live in East Anglia, and how far is it to the Silkeborg Museum? Six hundred miles as the crow flies? As far as Edinburgh and back. I have been to Edinburgh and back.

All this is not the point, though it is puzzling. What is wrong with me that I have not made the so small effort needed when the face of the Tollund Man is so central to my thoughts?

It is cold in East Anglia, windy cold, and I have knitted myself a balaclava to keep my neck and ears and head warm when I walk the dog. As I pass the mirror in the hall on the way out of the door, I notice myself in profile and I think how like my grandmother I have become. And, being like my grandmother, my face has become the face of the Tollund Man. The same hollowness of cheek, the same beakiness of nose. As if I have been preserved for two thousand years and am still continuing to be. Is it possible, do you think, that I belong, through whatever twisted threads, to the family of the Tollund Man? I'm not trying to make myself special in any way, you understand. There must be other people of the family; thousands of them. I see other people of my age, on buses, or walking their dogs, or waiting for their grandchildren to choose an ice cream from the van, who have the same contours to their faces, the same blend of peacefulness, humanity and pain. There are far more who have none of these things, though. Whose faces are careless or undefined or pinched or foolish.

The truth is, I do want to be special. I want there to be significance in the connection made between you and me in 1964 and links back to the man buried in the bog two thousand years ago. I am not very coherent. Please do not bother to reply if you think I do not justify your time.

Yours sincerely,
T. Hopgood (Mrs)

Silkeborg Museum
Denmark
10th December

Dear Mrs Hopgood,
I refer to your letter addressed to Professor Glob. Professor Glob died in 1985. If he had still been alive, he would by now be 104 years old, which is not impossible, but is unlikely.

I believe you are asking two questions in your letter:

i. Is there any reason why you should not visit the museum?

ii. Is there any possibility you are distantly related to the Tollund Man?

In answer to the first, I would encourage you to make the effort, which need not be very great, to visit us here. There are regular flights from Stansted, or, if you prefer, from Heathrow or Gatwick, to Aarhus airport, which is the most convenient for arriving in Silkeborg. The museum is open every day between 10 and 5, except in winter when it opens only at the weekends from 12 until 4. Here you can see the Elling Woman as well as the Tollund Man and an exhibition looks at all aspects of those who lived in the Iron Age; for instance, what they believed in, how they lived, how they mined and worked the mineral that gives the period its name. I must also correct something you said in your letter. Although only the head of the Tollund Man is preserved, the rest of the body has been re-created so the figure you will see, if you visit us here, will look just as it did when it was recovered from the bog, including the hands and the feet.

In answer to your second question, the Centre for Geo-Genetics at our Naturhistorisk Museum is at the moment trying to extract some DNA from the Tollund Man's tissues, which would help us to understand his genetic links to the present day population of Denmark. You will have read, in Professor Glob's book, that the index finger of the Tollund Man's right hand shows an ulnar loop pattern which is common to 68 per cent of the Danish people, which gives us confidence that this study will find such links. Through the Vikings, who came later to Denmark but will have inter-bred with the existing population, there is most likely some commonality of genes to the population of the UK. So, I would say, it is quite possible that there is a family connec-tion, however slight, between yourself and the Tollund Man.

I hope this information is helpful to you, and look forward to meeting you if you visit us here.

Regards,
The Curator

Bury St Edmunds
6th January

Dear Mr Curator,

It was generous of you to reply to my letter to Professor Glob, and to try to answer what you understood my questions to be. But they were not questions. The reason I have not visited has nothing to do with the problems of travel. I have passed my sixtieth birthday but am nonetheless quite fit. I could go tomorrow. There have been few times in my life when that has not been so. Leaving aside childbirth and a broken leg, I have always been physically able to climb onto a plane, or indeed a ferry, to Denmark.

This being the case, I am forced to consider what might be the real reasons, because your answer to an unasked question has made me want to be honest with myself. Please be aware, I am writing to you to make sense of myself. You do not need to concern yourself with any of this. I do not expect you to reply.

My best friend at school was called Bella. This was not her given name and is not the name in Professor Glob's dedication: it is a nickname, based on her ability to pronounce Italian words. She was rubbish at languages, as far as learning to use them to communicate was concerned, but she could act them beautifully. Her favourite word was *bellissima*. She was able to put a level of meaning into each syllable which varied according to the context so the word seemed to mean more, when she said it, than it actually does. In fact, everything she said had more meaning, more intensity, than the same words used by anyone else.

We were friends from the first day we met, which was our first day at school. She was more colourful than I was;

adventurous, alive in the moment. She brought me energy and confidence and I loved her for it. What she loved about me, I think, was the steadiness. I was always there, always had a hand ready to hold hers. We were friends all our lives. All her life, for I am still alive, as you know, and she is not. And all our lives we talked about the time when we would visit the Tollund Man. We were, you see, always going to do it, but not yet. To begin with, we did not want to use up this treat before we had savoured the looking forward to it. We were maybe, also, a little afraid that it would not be what we had hoped. We hoped it would be significant in some way – we could not have told you in what way – and there was a risk it would not be. Our school friends went, helter-skelter. As soon as *The Bog People* was published in translation, if not before. They came back with an even stronger sense of ownership of the Tollund Man and Professor Glob and all things Danish than they already had. Bella and I thought they were superficial and unworthy and that the experience they had had was trivial, in comparison to the experience we would have. One day.

Then before it was quite the right time, we both made the mistake of getting married too young. I married the father of the child I was expecting, and became bogged down, almost literally, in the life of a farmer's wife. I have had opportunities enough to ponder on the centuries the Tollund Man spent in the peat, following seams of different coloured silt on the cut edge of a dyke and wondering which of these I would choose as mattress and duvet for a long, long sleep. My life has been a buried one. Bella's mistake was quite different. She married an Italian. I sometimes think that if we hadn't given her the nickname, she would not have married him. He was a clever, manipulative man. I used to feel, after I had spent any time with him, as if I had been eating cream cakes and ice-skating both at once. He overwhelmed Bella. He wore her away and when she was paper-thin and empty, he went back to Italy with their child, with her child. It doesn't seem impossible, does it, for a woman to regain a daughter who has gone no further than Milan? But it was. So many people became involved, pulling in different directions, each with a determination to win, one way or another. Every one of these agencies – the Catholic Church, the courts, the Social Services – was positive their view was the right one. I have never been that certain of anything, myself. After a decade the Italian factions won a final victory and Bella went to live in Italy, too, to be near her daughter.

During the decade before she left, in the darkest times, one of us would suggest we go to Denmark, and the other would veto it. I would say: 'If we just once saw the face of the Tollund Man, we might borrow some of his calmness.'

She would say: 'The point of the Tollund Man is the long view. Centuries passing. I can't take the long view.'

Or she would say: 'I can't stand this any longer. Let's go to Denmark. We might feel as we did when we were girls, full of hope.'

I would say: 'We're not girls, though, are we, and we need to see this through before we start letting ourselves look towards better times.'

When it was all over, I stayed at home, with the stock and the crops and my own children. We saw each other, of course, travelled back and forth, but the cares of middle life made us ordinary. We thought and worried and talked about all the things that seem important when the time ahead and the time behind are more or less in balance. Money, health, appearance, partners, children. We hardly mentioned the Tollund Man in this time, though I think we both understood that we still expected to visit him, and that we would both know when the right time had come.

When Bella came back from Italy, she fell ill. She was in and out of hospital, undergoing this treatment and that treatment and always, always talking about when she got better. This time we did plan. We did look up the ways to travel, calculated the cost, worked out an itinerary. It felt as if we were about to complete a circle, reaching out to the Tollund Man at the end of our lives as we had at the beginning. Holding out a hand to a hand preserved from the past, hoping to be part of a chain that in some way preserved us into the future.

She died before we could come to you. I don't know if I will be able to make the journey without her. I never planned to do that.

Sincerely,

Tina Hopgood

Silkeborg
20th January

Dear Mrs Hopgood,

Thank you for your letter, and of course I realise my answers were not the answers you were looking for. My business is facts. I collect and catalogue facts and artefacts, from which the facts are deduced, relating to the life and times of Iron Age man. My greatest pleasure in the work I do is to speculate on the facts we do not know, because time has eroded all evidence. But this is not, strictly, my job.

I am sure you will forgive me if I point out those parts of your letter that do not altogether agree with the facts as we know them. First, you speak of choosing strata in the layers of the soil in Suffolk (you use a striking image to describe this, which I would never have thought of myself) as a final resting place like the Tollund Man's grave. I have researched the soil composition in your part of East Anglia and find it is principally chalky clay left behind by the last period of glaciation, with some lighter, sandy deposits associated with river valleys. Although your country still has peat bogs, I do not believe that any of them are close to where you live. The Tollund Man was found between two layers of peat and I think you would be unlikely to locate such a bed for your final sleep on your husband's farm.

There were, of course, Iron Age settlements in your area of England. You might like to visit Warham Camp, a well-preserved earthwork, or Grimes Graves.

I am concerned not to upset you, as I see the death of your friend has been difficult, but I also need to correct any assumption you may have made about the Tollund Man 'choosing' where his body was left and, eventually, found. The practice at this time, during the early Iron Age, around 600–300 BC, was for bodies to be cremated. This was done with some ceremony and we can assume that it was felt to confer honour on the dead and a safe passage into the next world. Once the body had been burnt, the bones were picked out of the ashes and placed in urns or wrapped in cloth and then buried, often with a small piece of metal – a brooch or an ornament – and it is these remains, in funeral mounds, that allow us to speak with confidence of the way the dead were treated.

The Tollund Man did not die a natural death and was, as we know, not cremated. He was buried in a place far from any habitation in the middle of an area that had been recently exploited for fuel, something we can be sure was precious to the people among whom he lived. The average temperatures were 2–3°C below what they are today and Denmark, even now, can have many nights at below -10°C in the winter. Fuel would also have been necessary to cook the vegetable grains into a porridge; we know this was the diet of the time from the contents of the stomachs of the peat bog bodies and other evidence. The men of that time were in awe of the bogs. They were places of mystery; not land, not water, but something in between, and the Tollund Man would not have seen such a place as somewhere peaceful to lie down for his final rest. This is all very dry and dull, I am sure, and I wish I had the skill to move at once, and more elegantly, to the point I am trying to make. The Tollund Man, I believe, was a sacrifice intended to please whatever power provided the peat.

Now, to the matter of your so-long-delayed visit. You mention your husband and children. If you do not wish to make the journey alone, could you not come with some member of your family? I have children myself – my wife, alas, is not with me any more – and they will usually do something with me I do not care to do alone. They humour me, I think is the English expression. It would be a pleasure to me to show you the museum, if you could find a way of making the trip.

Regards,
Anders Larsen, Curator

Bury St Edmunds
9th February

Dear Mr Larsen,

It is so kind of you to carry on writing to me. I find it is one of the benefits of growing older, that people tend to be kind – to pick up the things I drop, for example, or remain patient in the queue behind me when I can't get my gloves off to open my purse to pay for the things I am trying to buy. But you can't see me; you are being kind to an unknown correspondent. So, thank you. You have also told me some things I did not know, and I am ashamed of myself. I have lived all my life in this landscape and have never understood its nature except in such superficial aspects as its stickiness, bleakness, ability to grow raspberries, inability to grow rhododendrons. I have never visited any Iron Age sites; I am going to, though. Truly. I have a date marked in the calendar when I can be spared and I will go on that date, no matter what.

Knowing as much as you do about those who lived long before us in unimaginably different circumstances, and who have left so little, but that little so significant – knowing all this, do you not stumble over your own unimportance? I wish the English language had some impersonal pronoun, like 'one', which no one uses any more, because that last sentence reads as if I am attributing a lack of importance just to you. To you, Anders Larsen, Curator at Silkeborg Museum, when what I want to say is, wouldn't anyone feel how paltry their life is, knowing what you (and I mean you, here) know?

You mentioned that I was upset at Bella's death. It's true, I was. I still miss her and grieve for her, but, you know, she is so completely gone – cremated, as you tell me the Tollund Man's contemporaries were – and scattered as ashes, leaving

11

not a trace behind. In contrast to Bella, the bog people are as if newly dead, hardly dead at all, but resting in plain sight, bearing witness to their having been, having lived.

I am making no sense at all and will stop writing.

Best wishes,

Tina Hopgood

Silkeborg
21st February

Dear Mrs Hopgood,

Do not feel you must stop writing. Your letters are making me think, and I am enjoying this thinking, so please do not stop writing. In particular, I have been thinking of what it is that makes history, the sort of history that is my special field. What lasts? What is it that determines what lasts?

I thought first of violence. The Tollund Man and the other bog people died violent deaths. If there had been no violence, their bodies would have been burned, like the bodies of all the other people who lived at the same time. Also, if I look at the artefacts we have from the time in which they lived, I see how many of these are to do with killing. Perhaps this is why we feel ourselves (I feel as you imagine I would) to be un-important. Because we do not live by, and are unlikely to die by, violence. This must be good. I will accept insignificance in exchange for a peaceful life.

My second thought is beauty. Some of the other surviving objects are everyday and ordinary and have been preserved by accident. But most of them are beautiful. They were put in graves because they were the best. Or they were preserved as objects of religious significance and had been crafted with the most care and attention to beauty as a tribute to the gods.

The preservation of an object of beauty carries meaning, I think, beyond the physical appearance, to those who look at it and handle it after those who first made it and owned it are gone. I am brought to this opinion not only because of what I feel, and notice the visitors feel, when looking at a neck torc or a fertility amulet. When my wife died, she left me a bracelet we had bought together on our honeymoon in Venice, a simple, silver circle with a delicate pattern engraved on the surface; a thing to be held and touched and studied closely for its beauty to be understood. I study it now she has gone because I have no place where I can visit and believe myself to be close to her. No grave, no urn, no place where ashes were scattered. So I see this circle as being the link between us even though we are forever apart. I mention this only in support of my beauty theory. There is no reason I could not have picked a hairbrush or a glove or a keyring, something else she touched thousands of times in her life, as the amulet to keep her close to me. But the bracelet is beautiful, as these other things are not.

Please forgive me this intrusion of my personal affairs into our correspondence.

Regards,
Anders Larsen

Bury St Edmunds
6th March

Dear Mr Larsen,

There is nothing to forgive. I have been personal, too. I am also enjoying the thinking so I will go on writing, hoping you will reply; but I would not be offended if you do not.

I do not agree with you about violence. I live with violence and it is diminishing. Of course, the maiming and killing that are a regular part of my life involve animals, not humans. But it is violence, nonetheless.

When I was first married, the pigs were killed on the farm. The slaughterman was the husband of the landlady of the local pub and was shaped like a spider: short, round body; long arms and legs. He was set in a crouching position through years of heaving barrels up and down cellar steps and man-handling live and dead carcasses. He had no teeth and smelt of blood and slops and sweat. If anyone lived by violence, he did. Yet he is dead now and if I mentioned his name in the village shop, they would remember him only after a pause for thought, or not at all.

The pigs to be slaughtered were driven into a pen outside a shed in the yard. I don't suppose you've ever had much to do with a live pig; they are intelligent animals, but physically incompetent. They are ridiculously easy to steer – it only takes a board held against the side of the head to guide them in the direction you want them to go. They have such limited ability to see in any plane except straight ahead that it is as though the world ceases to exist for them when they cannot see it. We have a phrase in English: 'like a lamb to slaughter', which means an innocent who is manipulated towards disaster. I have always thought this saying should describe a pig, because lambs are actually less easy to lead to their deaths than pigs are.

I find myself wondering if this is how the Tollund Man went to his death. I look at his face (in photographs, of course) and imagine he must have, pig-like, allowed himself to be led to the bog and the rope, worrying about nothing except sticking to a straight line. Was there, do you think, an executioner, in the bog? A man who had been chosen or put himself forward for the job of sacrificing the man who was chosen or put himself forward as the offering to the gods? I know, I know, you deal in facts derived from objects and physical evidence. You were not there; no one who was there created an account, how can we ever know?

It is not violence, I would say, but sacrifice that is the key. Look at all the saints. They sacrificed themselves for their faith and are consequently part of the currency of life centuries later: in the religious calendar, in the paintings and sculptures in every gallery; on postcards; commemorated in the naming of churches, streets, squares, buildings. Of course the sacrifice has to be worthwhile, as the saints' and the Tollund Man's were, in the context of the time they lived in. It was a sacrifice to something greater than themselves.

I feel I have sacrificed my life, too, but for nothing. I have sacrificed myself, firstly, to the social standards of my parents and their peers, which prohibited me from having an abortion, or having a baby and remaining single. Secondly, I sacrificed myself to the farm. My husband – his name is Edward – is satisfied as long as he has the land, the crops, the stock and the jobs to be done in each season as it comes around. I am not, but because the seasons come round so relentlessly and the jobs are so many, I cannot escape. It is so long since the sacrifice was made, I was so young at the time, it took so many years for me to realise I had made it, that I can no longer say what, exactly, it was that I sacrificed; what it was that would have given me the satisfaction Edward feels every day. Perhaps it was the trip to Denmark – that could have been enough. But the blank space in my life is too great to be overwritten by so slight an act.

I do not want to sound as if I am full of self-pity. I am not. I have had my moments of joy; we have had fun together, Edward and I, and are drifting towards old age in harmony. I have children and grandchildren and they have brought me happiness. But first to not-quite-last, what is it that I have missed by having closed off so many choices so early in my life?

I have just looked up from the page, and seen, through the window, my youngest grandchild, a little girl not yet three years old, running across the yard and stopping to poke her glove through the cover of a drain. She is at the age when to squat is as easy as to sit down on a chair (too long ago for me to remember) and she almost has the glove past the bars when her father, my son Tam, comes into sight and catches her up. He wipes her hands on his overalls and carries her off. She is squealing as the pig squealed. This has made me smile, has made me happy for an instant.

But tell me more about your wife. I want to know why you have no grave, no urn and no ashes.

Best wishes,

Tina Hopgood

Silkeborg
21st March

Dear Mrs Hopgood,

The story of why I have no grave and no urn or ashes is not an easy one for me to tell and I will save it for a later letter, perhaps, if you continue to write to me as I hope you will, or maybe, even until you visit the museum here in Silkeborg, and we meet, face to face. I can see the Tollund Man every day, if I choose, and like you, I am always moved by his look of calm. You should visit.

Your last letter made me realise how different our lives have been. This needs some explanation, because of course our experience would appear to be so very similar; we were both born into a post-war world and have known no conflict; we both married, had children; we have endured no physical hardship. But my life has been devoted to the past, to small and unchanging man-made objects. When I wake in the night and wonder if, after all, I have wasted my chances and should have done something different with the time and the talents I have been given, I am often terrified by how small are the things I study and how big and beyond understanding is everything they represent.

Now you, on the other hand, have lived in the great space of the natural world, where everything changes. I mean the seasons, the soil, the business of sowing, growing and harvesting, of animal fertility and its consequences. I wonder, when you wake in the night, are you also terrified by the greatness of what you have to deal with, day by day? Or is it so commonplace for you that you feel no fear?

Do you wake terrified? I assume everyone does, at some time. My wife did, often, when she was alive, and I would wake to comfort her. She was never boring, my wife, never ordinary. When we talked about our fears and dreams, she made me feel in touch with what was otherwise just outside my reach. Now she is gone and I have no one else I can talk to about such things.

I end, as always, with an apology. This is not why you started this correspondence, to read about my views on ideas too grand for me to be able to express them as I would like to do, even if my English, like yours, was perfect.

Best wishes,

Anders Larsen

Bury St Edmunds
2nd April

Dear Mr Larsen,

You are wrong, I started this correspondence because I am plagued by the same thoughts you have just so succinctly, and in excellent English, expressed. But my response to you on this subject must, like the story of your wife, wait for another letter because, first, I have a story to tell you. I have been on a journey. I said I would visit an Iron Age site in East Anglia, and I have. On the day I circled in my diary. This might seem like a small boast. I decided which day to go and I went, on that day. It is more of an achievement for me than it seems. I have the idea that other people manage their lives like a set of interlocking boxes, each piece fitted snugly to the next (like your Danish Lego, I realise, as I write this, though what was in my mind was something more crafted, less engineered and colourful), and they can move from box to box in full control and with complete confidence that it is the right time to leave one box and enter another. My life is more like a pile of timber. Random.

Anyway, I went to Warham Camp Iron Age Hill Fort. It is about fifty miles from where I live and I drove myself there. I did investigate buses because I prefer a journey to feel like a journey rather than a trip to the shops, but it would have been impossible to arrange within the tottering pile of planks that I had to negotiate to make it out of the house for that long, at that particular moment. By the time I had cooked breakfast, fed the hens, dealt with the eggs and prepared lunch, it would have been too late to set off. So I went by car. I was going to plunge in with my impressions of Warham Camp, which are batting about in my brain demanding to be set down. But I will restrain myself, so you can see it as I saw it, having travelled there.

It was a lovely day; enough of a wind and a frost to give it bite, blue sky and sunshine enough to give it sparkle. I was troubled by the sun in my eyes on the drive up there, kept having to manipulate the visor to block it out. I am not the sort of woman (and I suspect you would know this without my telling you) who owns a pair of sunglasses. I do not own a satellite navigation system, either, but I had memorised the names of the places I would need to pass through to reach Warham – Thetford, Swaffham, Little Walsingham – and arrived safely.

I parked in the village. There were no road markings but a woman came out of the house alongside the verge where I had parked and I thought at once that she had come to upbraid me for leaving my car there. Edward and Tam, my husband and eldest son, are forever alert to anyone who seems to be treating any inch of our four hundred acres as if they had a right to it. The footpaths that run across it are a constant affront to them, and they know the rules for what you can and can't do on a footpath to the lowest sub-clause. So I thought the woman had come to tell me that it was her right to enjoy the view from her garden without the inconvenience of my car in the foreground.

'Is it all right to leave my car here?' I asked.

'Of course,' she said. 'There are no restrictions.' And she set about pruning her roses, which was clearly what she had come out of the house to do. I asked her the way to Warham Camp. She came over and waved her secateurs in the direction I should take. She told me that, if I was interested in ancient earthworks, I should also go to Fiddler's Hill Barrow.

'There is nothing in either place except mounds of earth covered in grass,' she said. 'But each of them is a pretty spot, and it's the perfect day for it.'

I set off. I had everything I needed in a little backpack one of my children once used as a school bag, and I thought it was making me stand up straighter than I would normally do, and that made me stand up straighter still and raise my head, and that made me look at everything around me as if I would be sitting an exam later on what I had seen. As I am, in a way. Please take this letter as my exam text. Mark with red ink and a score out of ten.

It was a narrow lane and no cars drove past me, just a squadron of cyclists, in Lycra, talking to each other. I began to anticipate what I would see when I reached the place and realised I had no idea what to expect, though I had researched it on the internet. I began to fear that my expectations were too high and I was bound to be disappointed.

I came to a little bridge and stopped to watch the water passing underneath it. Three women walked past me, travelling in the same direction as I was. They had walking boots and sticks and the kind of jacket that is designed for the outdoors and costs more than a sensible man would spend. This last phrase is my husband's and it leapt into my mind, not because I felt it right to condemn these women, but to stop myself feeling inadequate, with the zip-up boots I wear to go out and feed the chickens, a child's rucksack and an old quilted anorak with the stuffing poking through where I have caught it on pieces of wire. One of the women also had a rucksack, with many pockets, some of them mesh, and was tall and sturdy. The second woman was small and pretty. The third was skinny and ugly and had an unfortunate pair of trousers that were too wide and too short.

'Beautiful day,' said the tall one as they walked past. I let them walk on a little way before I followed. I thought that they, like me, must be going to Warham Hill Fort and I was cross. I had come here with the intention of feeling close to the people who lived here long ago; kindred, it might be, to the Tollund Man. Now I was going to have to share the place with three women who, I imagined, were simply ticking it off in a thoughtless way, adding it to the list of significant places visited. I desperately, at that moment, wanted to have Bella with me. Someone who would understand the mess of ideas in my head leading me to think this journey was an important one, to visit an earthy mound in the middle of nowhere. Unlike the women ahead of me, Bella would not be wearing the right shoes (not just on this occasion, actually, but pretty well always, Bella could be relied on to be wearing something on her feet completely at odds with the occasion). I wanted to be able to say 'Look at that' to someone beside me, and to know she would understand what I meant, even when there was nothing to see.

'I'm looking,' Bella might have said. 'All I can see is blades of grass but these are the blades of grass with our feet on, all four of our feet. Let's wriggle our toes.'

And then I thought, if not now, then later I could say 'Look at that' to you, in a letter. I hope you do not think it is presumptuous, casting you in the role of a substitute for the woman who was my best friend, but writing to you has begun to feel like talking to her.

The road passed alongside a ploughed field and from habit I paused to see if I could identify the crop that had been drilled in it. (A cereal, too early to tell what.) By the time I reached the entrance to Warham Camp, the women were out of sight. The path to the site had hedges on either side and the frost had stayed on the grass; I could still see the imprint of their boots. I chose a route nearer the hedge where their feet had not been, and tried to hold myself as if I felt I had more right to be there than the better-dressed women ahead of me.

But when I came out into the amphitheatre – is that the right word? – it mattered not one jot that there were other people, other living people, there with me. It felt like a place for the living, when I had expected it to feel like a crypt in a church, where the dead take precedence over those of us still travelling. I don't know what it was – the burst of sky, the rabbit scrapes and molehills, the turf-covered banks so neat yet natural, as if the men who had created them might at any moment come over the ridge with their scythes or shovels or flocks of sheep.

You will tell me – you who know so much – that of course

it is not a place of the dead. It is not a burial ground or barrow but somewhere people lived. I had been thinking too much, preparing for the visit, making the journey, about the buried past, and here I was standing where people had lived, and I had not thought about that at all. The ridges on the side of the earthworks were like benches where folk could sit, and I did. I sat down and began to imagine what might have occurred within the space before me and at once realised I didn't know. I had been so eager to come, so certain I would be moved by it, I had not taken the trouble to find out any facts. I took off my rucksack and took out the printouts from the internet. It felt altogether wrong to be sitting on such a day in such a place and looking all the while at a piece of paper. I understood, as I had not done before, how my husband Edward feels. He will never turn to the written word to find out what he wants to know. He would rather trust in instinct, experience, the texture of the soil, the direction of the wind, the few words of advice from a fellow farmer. Our son Tam, who farms the land with him, reads all the agricultural papers and tries to interest his father in what they have to say, but Edward says:

'Oh, yes, and how many signs did you miss while you had your eyes fixed downwards on the writing?'

It was one of the things I only learnt about him after marriage, that he saw no sense in reading, and I wondered how we would ever be able to live together, being so different, but now, forty years later, I could understand what he means by that sort of remark. I wanted to be able to look about me and learn from what I saw, not from what I read. But I had no experience, and no friend, to help me read the signs, so I scrabbled about for my reading glasses. The skinny, plain woman came up and stood nearby. I caught her eye and she commented on the beauty of the day as her friend had done earlier. I abandoned the hunt for my glasses. She looked unhealthy, close up, despite the outdoor gear. Her face was the colour and texture and not far off the shape of a beet dug up from the ground in the middle of winter.

'I've never been here before,' I said. 'I read up about it before I came but now I don't remember what I read.'

'I know it well,' she said. 'I studied archaeology. Tell me what you want to know and I'll see if I can help.'

So, you see, there was an alternative to a piece of paper. A passing archaeologist, called Marion. She sat on the bank beside me and she told me about the site, and then about herself.

I felt, as she spoke, that the Iron Age and Roman peoples were moving all around me, going about the business of cooking and washing and creating domestic objects as I do. As if it could at once be two thousand years in the past but also two thousand years in the future, when some other pair of strangers meet where I live now and recognise the life I led, from the pieces of my best green Denby plates and a rusty but recognisable size-8 knitting needle. Some of the things that were found at Warham Camp, Marion said, were discovered in molehills or when rabbits eroded the bank, and some of it when men arrived to dig with the purpose of finding things. I was taken with this idea, of the earth as a barrel of apples, where day by day hands reach in and take out the fruit at the top for immediate use, and refill it for tomorrow, but once in a while a curious hand will delve beneath the top layer, or a rat will creep in through a crack in the planking and disturb the lower levels so the older apples come up into the light, in all their strange and forgotten variety. It makes farming seem much closer to the work you do. It is about picking up and replacing the top layer; yours are the hands that go deeper.

Marion and the other women were not, as I assumed, lifelong friends with successful careers whose relaxation is walking together. They met at sessions arranged for women recovering from breast cancer and agreed to do something, each month, to help them keep in focus the miracle of being alive. The group, Marion told me, was once larger than it is now. I wished Bella had met these women, when she was going through what they have been through. But as soon as I had this thought, I knew Bella would not have been able to join them. She was too snappy, too angry. I do not know how I would react, in the circumstances they are in, but I suspect I would collapse into the arms of their friendship easily enough. I hope I would.

Now I think – having written the paragraph above – did your wife die of this disease? Can you bear to read no further? If you do not write again, I will understand, though just thinking this makes me feel a sense of loss greater than I would have expected.

The others came up and we took our flasks of coffee from our rucksacks and shared our biscuits, then they set out to walk back to Warham and I carried on down the lanes to Fiddler's Hill Barrow, which was an earthy mound, as predicted.

Marion had told me the site could have origins dating back to before the Iron Age, and the barrow would have been used to bury the dead, or the ashes of cremated bodies, for centuries after that. I felt as I had expected to feel, when I went to Warham Camp, as if I could put my hand on the turf and imagine the bones of other hands piled up far below, but somehow still within reach. Only it was cold, and I was hungry and there was almost nothing to see, so I walked briskly back down the lanes to Warham and went to the pub for a bowl of soup.

The woman whose house I was parked beside was serving behind the bar. She asked if I had found the Camp and if I had gone on to Fiddler's Hill. Yes, I said, and yes. She apologised for having sent me to the barrow.

'After you'd gone, I remembered it could hardly be called a pretty spot, even in winter. The council has planted an orchard of ancient varieties of apple trees there, but they're just so many bare branches at this time of year.'

To make up for any disappointment I might have felt about the actual place, she told me the story of how it got its name. Legend has it that a tunnel was found, running from a village called Blakeney to the priory in Binham, the next village to Warham. No one was brave enough to go down it, except for a fiddler, who set off with his dog, playing a tune as he went. The worthies of the district followed above ground, guided by the sound of the fiddle until, just where Fiddler's Hill is today, it stopped. They assumed that the devil had got him and his dog, and built a mound to mark the spot. Between the wars, the rose-pruning barmaid told me, the barrow was cut away to widen the road, and they found the skeletons of three humans and – she leant forward and lowered her voice – a dog.

'No sign of a fiddle?' I asked.

'Not that I heard.'

The tunnel, I imagine, would be low and the fiddler entering it bent to half a normal man's height, and for this reason, I see the fiddler in my mind as the hunchbacked slaughterman I told you about who came to kill the pigs. He was the kind of man to go fearlessly ahead, with a kind of obstinate stupidity, when other men hung back.

I have no more to tell you about my journey. Next time I will be brisk, and more coherent, because this has been a self-indulgent meander and I am sorry to have put you to the trouble of reading it (if you do). I am not sorry to have written it, so at least one of us had some enjoyment out of all these words.

All the best,
Tina

Silkeborg
13th April

Dear Mrs Hopgood,

Reading your letter, I wondered whether I should not visit your country to see for myself the evidence of the Iron Age that remains in the landscape, just as you have wondered about visiting my country to see the remains of an Iron Age man. I was sorry not to have been the passing archaeologist who gave you information but you are there and I am here and I do not know what she told you. So I will write my own guide for your next visit. This is very arrogant of me because I am not an expert on the Iceni tribe who lived in the area during the late Iron Age. Also, no one knows the answers to the question I imagine you might have wanted to ask, that is: what was life like for the men, women and children who lived inside the fortified ditches of the Fort? I am used to facts, based on evidence. I will give you what facts I can and you must imagine, for both of us, how it must have been.

The people in Warham Hill Fort at the time the Tollund Man was alive near the bog in Bjaeldskov Dal would have lived in circular huts with walls formed around upright poles and a roof supported by rafters reaching down to touch the ground. This is very different from the settlement the Tollund Man would have lived in; here in Denmark they built long-houses, big rectangles with space at one end for men, women and children, and room at the other for beasts. In the round huts built in Britain at the time, a man could stand upright only in the centre, and this is where family life would have taken place – cooking, eating, sewing, mending tools and such other activities as might have been normal in a home at this time. Around the edges of the hut were the sleeping quarters, and storage areas, tucked in below and between the rafters.

I do not know how big the community of the Fort was, but there would have been several families, maybe thirty huts. These forts existed because there was land enough to support such a body of people, not primarily for defensive purposes, though attacks were always possible. The people in such communities led a settled, agricultural life; you were right to imagine men with scythes and sheep coming over the embankment towards you. In the fields round about they grew cereal in the summer, ploughing the ground with the help of oxen, harvesting the corn with scythes and drying it for storing in the winter. They kept cattle for meat, as well as to pull the plough, and for leather for clothes and other uses around the farm. We have evidence that beef was commonly eaten. We also have evidence that sheep were kept by inhab-itants of settlements like this, but less evidence that mutton was eaten. We can assume they were kept mainly for wool;

weaving, alongside the production of pottery, was one of the most common crafts. The animals will have been taken to graze further off in the summer, but brought back to fertilise and turn over the soil of the fields in winter.

Most of the people living in Warham Hill Fort will have been subject to the authority of an overlord, a wealthy man with his attendant warriors who was able to lay claim to enough land to produce food for himself and his family and to support the labour needed to make it productive. There was a hierarchy, with the workers – the peasants – at the bottom. They could have been slaves, but even if notionally free, they would have had no alternative way to provide food and shelter for themselves than to labour in the service of the chieftain. He had a bigger hut, with an additional room or porch; he had finer goods and ornaments. Even in death, he was treated differently. He was buried, after cremation, in a grave dug with care, the ashes in an urn or ornate bucket, and items of value or of use in the afterlife buried with him, as if he was going to live all over again. The poor people's ashes were treated with less dignity, though all but the poorest would have had some items beautiful or useful put in the grave beside them.

The people of the Fort obeyed the chief in earthly matters, but their religious guides were the druids, who taught them to believe that there was an afterlife, which is why it was important to have beside you something to help you pass on to whatever the next life might be.

It is hard to find evidence from archaeological artefacts for the life that women led in this society. However, after the Roman invasion, we have written observations. Caesar says, writing of the tribes in the areas the Romans first conquered in Britain, that wives would be shared by groups of ten or twelve men, in a family group, so the brothers, father or sons of the man who took a woman into his home could also treat her as a wife. Any children she had, however, were counted as her husband's children, no matter who the father might have been. Husbands, according to Caesar, held a right of life or death over their wives. But then Boudicca was queen of the Iceni tribe, and she led her tribe into battle against the Romans, so the women in Warham Camp may not have been so subject to their husbands' rule.

I am afraid of wearying you with so much detail that I am not expressing in an interesting way. So I will stop. I have one last thing to say about your trip, though. In Denmark, I do not think the woman who saw you sitting alone on the grassy bank would have come to speak to you. Most Danes, I believe, would have thought you were solitary because you chose to be, and would have respected that. Maybe this lady – Marion – should have respected your privacy, and maybe you hoped she would, but I am pleased she became part of the story; it would have been less of a story – less of an important journey – if you had not met her.

Thank you for sharing it with me.

Anders

Bury St Edmunds
20th April

Dear Anders,

I wish I had received your letter before I went to Warham Camp. As you say, what I really wanted to feel while I was there was how the people lived, what it would have been like for them to live there. Marion talked about the artefacts they made, but not how they lived, and now you have given me details that allow me to come closer to imagining this. Even if it isn't possible to describe an individual life lived in that place, I can now imagine what a woman, for example, standing at the entrance to her home, looking out to see if her husband or her children were in sight and safe, might have seen and heard and smelt. I can picture the team of oxen being driven out to the fields, pulling a plough behind them. In my mind I see, through a drifting smoke, mud, churned up with the passage of feet, animal and human. I hear the sounds men and cattle make, calling to each other, and the rattle and whir of whatever machinery is used to make the things they need, the cloth and the pots. There would have been children's voices. You do not mention toys, but there must, surely, have been games the children played, and things they made to play with? I expect the woman was blinking, in the light, after the dark of the hut, and I cannot help but feel she would have been anxious, as she looked and listened, alert for anything out of the ordinary. She would have smelt the smoke, and the organic waste of people and animals.

I imagined this woman as I walked out of my own house, the morning after I received your letter. The day was over-cast, with clouds banked up behind the barn, and although it was not yet raining, the light was dimmer outside the house than inside it. I came out, as I do every morning, to feed the chickens. Maybe she did, too. You don't mention poultry – maybe they left no trace, or maybe the strains of bird designed to feed people hadn't been developed. I'm not sure what my Iron Age woman would have been holding in her hands, but

31

I was carrying the feed in an old plastic bucket, which once held rat poison. Whatever she held, it would not have been plastic and it would not have had a previous purpose connected with a highly engineered approach to the elimination of rodents. Rodents, I should think, could have been one of the things she saw, as she stood in her hut doorway, and accepted as being inevitable. The yard outside my back door is concrete, and Edward is a careful farmer, so it is clean. I could hear a quad bike – Tam, who lives in a bungalow a couple of hundred metres away from the farmhouse, setting off to check on the sheep. Through the open door behind me, I could hear voices on a radio. Although Tam lives so close, and has two small children, I could not hear children; in this, the Iron Age woman's life was richer than mine. Although, when I look at my grandchildren, I love to see how each day is an adventure for them, whereas back then, I expect a mother or grandmother would have seen each day a child lived as a battle won. I could smell the honeysuckle growing over the garden wall and the gases given off by a trailer full of organic waste standing ready to be spread on the fields.

I must have been standing, holding the chicken feed bucket but not moving, for several minutes, because Edward came out and asked me what the matter was.

'Nothing,' I said. 'I'm just having a look round.'

He stood beside me, and we both looked round for a while longer. He pointed out the gutter on a cart shed that needed fixing, and a patch of nettles overdue for an application of weedkiller.

'It's a good idea to just stand and look, sometimes,' he said.

Edward is much closer to Iron Age man than I am to Iron Age woman. He lives exactly in the moment, as they must have done.

I still know nothing about your wife.

Best wishes,

Tina

Silkeborg
2nd May

Dear Tina,

I went outside my house, the morning after I received your letter, and looked around. I have no chickens to feed and, usually, I do not go outside until it is time to go to work, and then I am thinking only of whether I have forgotten anything and whatever it is I have to do when I arrive. This was new for me, to go outside before breakfast, just to see what is outside.

I have a hedge between my house and the road, which is green now but bronze in winter. I noticed it needed to be trimmed; this is a householder's thought and I wanted to look not as a householder, so I walked to the pavement. Even then, I realised, I could see little. Most of my neighbours have hedges. Although I live on a small hill above the lakes of Silkeborg, I could not see them. I found I was noticing that the surface of the road is broken and needs repair, so I looked upwards instead. The sky was magnificent. I have always loved the sky and I do not take notice of it often enough.

I could hear almost nothing. The sound of a neighbour's flag flapping against the pole. In the distance was a light hum of traffic, but nothing close to me. A bird was singing. I could not have named it from the song. I do not think I would have known what it was if I had been able to see it. I could not hear children. In Denmark today the children go to nursery, paid for by the state, when they are only one year old or so, and unless I happen to be passing a school or a nursery during break time, in sunny weather when the children are playing outside, I never do hear them. Through my open door I could hear the music I had put on when I came downstairs. Shostakovich. The only thing I could smell was my own coffee, although I find smells hide themselves from me unless I have not smelt them for some time. Then they remind me of themselves.

No one came out of any of the houses. This is a good neighbourhood and I know and like my neighbours, but as I stood there, thinking about you standing in your farmyard imagining an Iron Age settlement, I thought how private we have all become. How self-sufficient. Of course, we are all members of whatever society we live in, but not in the way the Tollund Man's contemporaries would have been members of the community he lived in. They would have been cogs, wheels, brackets, levers, pulleys, each making their society work according to their skills and position. Now we are like ball bearings, complete in ourselves and joining other ball bearings only to form shapes which suit our purpose.

When I went back into the house, the phone was ringing and it was my daughter calling from Copenhagen. I have not told you about my children, I think. I cannot tell you about my children without first telling you about my wife.

My wife did not die of breast cancer, and I did not stop

reading your earlier letter when you described the women who were friends because they had suffered this disease, but read to the end. You have a gift for finding joy in small moments, which is a thing I used to have, but have lost, and part of this is because of my wife's story, which is a sad one. Perhaps if I share it with you now, we can continue with our correspondence hereafter in a more joyous strain.

My wife's name was Birgitt. She was born in the city, in Copenhagen, but when she was five or six, her mother was no longer able to care for her. Birgitt remembered a time of half-light, of hunger and thirst, cold and damp. When her father came home from a business trip, so she learnt later, he found her mother had gone to the park and was sleeping on a bench. Birgitt was locked in the flat, the curtains drawn. She had made a nest under the table, where the cloth hung down almost to the floor. There was no food in the house. The radio had been left on, tuned to a classical music station. She could never afterwards listen to classical music, particularly the great symphonies, without crying.

Birgitt's mother was sent to a home in which she died, almost at once, or so Birgitt was led to believe, without once coming home to the flat with the table or seeing her child again. Birgitt was sent to live with her father's parents, on an island off the north-east corner of our country. Imagine the contrast. Just the view from the windows. All her life, she has seen other buildings and the tops of trees, with broken shapes of sky-colour in between. Now she can see only sky, and a flat landscape where nothing so large as a tree breaks the surface. Then her grandparents. Her mother allowed no routine. She slept and ate, went out and came in, at times she chose. When she was awake, and not eating, she would create for Birgitt.

I realise 'create' in English is a transitive verb, and needs to be followed by a noun (I had a very good teacher of English at my school), but it is hard for me to think of which noun to place after it. Games? Art? Food? Stories? All of these, but mostly she created a life that was not that of a mother and a six-year-old girl in a flat in Copenhagen.

The grandparents – Birgitt called them Ernst and Carla – had a life that was set as hard and fixed as the stones of the cottage they lived in. Every morning, they woke at the same time, went through the same steps to wash and dress, sat in the same seats to eat breakfast and so on throughout the day. Children are supposed to like to have a routine; it makes them feel safe. But Birgitt's routine had been to have no routine, and she was waiting all the time for something else to happen.

'When will it be different?' she asked her grandmother.

'Different to what?' Carla said.

'Just different.'

'Different in what way?' Her grandmother was a good and patient woman.

'Just different.'

It was not possible for them to understand that Birgitt did not know what alternative she was expecting. That was exactly the point. The unexpected.

The only unpredictable part of her new surroundings was the sea, and she became fascinated by it. Small as she was, she would trek over the rough grassland between her grandparents' cottage and the shore. Her mother had a passion for bright things and all the child's clothes were colours that were easy to see against the greys and greens and browns of the landscape, so Carla would let her go further than we might expect, so anxious are we now for the safety of the young. Birgitt said that one of the comforting things about the sea, apart from its constantly changing patterns, was the noise it made. In Copenhagen, there was noise. Here, there was none except the wind when it blew (which it usually did) and the surf breaking on the shore.

In Denmark the children go to school at seven, so Birgitt's first experience of school was on the island. This was another form of orderliness and another shock. She had not met many children and she was puzzled by how they were like her and yet not like her. I suppose all children have a sense of themselves as distinct from other children, but most of them will also have an idea of their relationship with a family or a community. They will understand where they fit. Birgitt did not fit.

Carla walked with her to the school, which was a mile away, each morning, and returned to fetch her in the afternoon. One afternoon, Birgitt was not there to be collected. The teacher said she had not been to school that day. Carla had left her at the door but Birgitt had not gone through it. It was Danish weather – you will know what I mean when I describe it for I expect you would recognise it as East Anglian weather. It was cool, windy, and the earth was dwarfed by the sky, huge and blue with clouds in turmoil. The whole village turned out to look for Birgitt, tripping over the grass on the dunes, wiping the sand out of their eyes and their hair, calling, calling. Nowadays half the houses on the shore would be empty except in high summer, but then there were people living in them and all those people came out too and searched outbuildings, looked under tarpaulins and behind sheds. Boats were launched and began searching the coast, the men and women holding the tillers looking fearfully at the surf and the breaking waves, as well as at the inlets and the safe, dry beaches. Darkness fell and the child had not been found.

There are a number of small islands in that part of Denmark, no more than rocks sticking up out of the sea. One of these is split from top to bottom, like a rack for a single piece of toast. At the bottom, the slit widens to make a cave, or would you call it a cove? Sheltered, with a sandy floor. The searchers found Birgitt in this place three days after she had last been seen. She was alone. There was food and blankets. She seemed not to have been harmed in any way.

The story she told was that a merman had invited her to go with him and she had gone. Had they swum to the island? the adults asked. No, she said. He had rowed the boat and she had guided him towards the rock. Every man who owned or could borrow a boat, and who was fit enough to row – that is almost the entire male population of the island where Birgitt lived – was interviewed. The child would not describe the man except to repeat that he was a merman, a sea creature, and it was impossible to link any of the men with the blankets and food on the rock. The search continued across the nearby mainland and many an innocent man in both communities had his innocence questioned and, maybe, was never quite believed to be innocent for the rest of his life. No one was ever arrested.

As an adult, Birgitt would admit that mermen do not exist and that whoever took her away in a boat was no more than a mortal with two legs. In her heart, though, she never believed it. This is not something she ever said, but I lived with her for thirty years and I loved her, so I feel justified in stating it to be so. She did not believe she was a part of the world as other people are a part of it. She was someone born to live alone, hidden away in small spaces, and the people who created these spaces were not made of the same matter as I am made of, and the rest of mankind. Her mother and the merman were real, to her, and the children and I were not. She played the game of happy families with us but we were toys; props to help her pretend to be like us. When the game became too much for her, she would leave us, for a few days, a week, once for over two months. I never knew where she went but I know what she was looking for. The door to the real world where the merman lived. As she grew older, the longing became stronger.

A couple of years ago we were on a ferry between Gothenburg and Frederikshavn. We were returning from a little holiday to celebrate our wedding anniversary. It was a stormy day: wind, rain, rough seas. Despite all this (because of all this?) my wife told me she wanted to go outside onto the deck; she felt nauseous, she said, from the noise and the smells on the inside of the boat. I said I would go with her but she said no, stay with the bags. As she left, she handed me the bracelet. She wore it always, but in her unhappiness she had become thin, and it was loose. She said:

'Keep this for me. It may slide from my wrist and I do not want it to be lost.'

I never saw her again. Her body has never been found. She left my side as if all her life she had been dreaming and now she wanted to wake to a new day.

I am surprised to find that I have never told this story before, not from start to finish as I have told you. I do not find it easy to speak of the things that affect me most deeply. But it is good to have told it. It is fixed now. A story that is over.

Your friend,

Anders Larsen

Bury St Edmunds
12th May

Dear Anders,

I want to go back to the letter you wrote to me in March before I say anything about your latest letter, because I will find it easier to speak of it if I approach it in this way.

You talked, in March, about the difference in our lives – mine in the midst of the landscape and change, yours caught up with objects fixed by time – and you asked, which is best and which would you have chosen, if you had known you had a choice? I know you did not ask this question any more than I asked the questions you answered in your first letter to me (how to get to Silkeborg, evidence of genetic links to Iron Age man) but I am putting it as a question because that is, precisely, the question I meant to ask you, or ask Professor Glob, as I thought at the time, when we began this correspondence. It is astonishing, is it not, that after I have led you, all uncomplaining, round the slaughter of pigs and the death of my best friend, you should have uncovered the real substance of what led me into the writing?

You ask whether I wake, terrified. I am not easily terrified, but after Bella died, I found I could not stop thinking, by day as well as by night, about what had become of my life, and there were moments when I felt the enormity of the might-have-been. She died in a hospice. If you don't have them in Denmark, you should. They make the going bearable for those who go and those who stay. You will understand, I see now, what a gift, what a boon that is. Her daughter, Alicia, was with her. So was I. Alicia is a girl with violent emotions. She shouts, if she is angry (and she is often angry), laughs and sings and dances when she is happy, and is loud and physical in grief. I love her for Bella's sake but she is exhausting. On the day Bella died, she behaved with dignity while the arrangements were made with the hospice staff, but as soon as we reached the car park, she became extreme. She ran round and round the parked cars, kicked the wall, all the time keeping up a wailing and a sobbing which must have been audible at Sainsbury's, a quarter of a mile away. We were also in full view of the hospice windows and I hate being a spectacle, so I sat in my car and waited for her to wear herself out.

There are moments, aren't there, when you pull some buried thought up to the forefront of your mind and realise you have been thinking this, without thinking it, for some while, and the time and place when this realisation occurs become a memory package, as it were, forever whole and capable of being recalled. Sitting in my car in the hospice car park, with Alicia racing back and forth like a pheasant startled by a dog, I began the process that led, in the end, to my first letter. Why had I led the life I had led, done so little, achieved so little. When my life is of such significance to me, how is it I could not claim any significance for it in the eyes of a disinterested observer? What life, if I had made a rational choice, would I have chosen? If I hadn't gone to the Young Farmers' disco and met Edward; if I had had less curiosity and animal appetite and had approached the business of sex more carefully? Though I doubt whether my choice would have been any more rational, if I had known I was making it. The obvious difference between my life and yours is that yours is mainly indoors and mine is substantially outside. Did you think about that when you were young? No, nor me. I don't know which I would have picked if I had put the alternatives to myself as a young girl. If I had recognised alternatives existed and I could select from among them. I know quite well that if I had led a life different from the one I have had, it would have been as the result of some urgent, momentary impulse as strong and as random as the one that made me Edward's wife and Tam's mother at the age of twenty. Who is to say that, whatever it might have been, that alternative life would not also have left me, as I sat in the hospice car park, with a sense of having been in the wrong room all my life, the room where nothing was happening?

Alicia stopped walking and sank down beside a BMW, sobbing like a child. I got out of the car, scooped her up and took her back to the flat where Bella had been living. She went into the bedroom and lay down on the bed with her face in the pillow and sobbed quietly but unendingly. The place was a mess, and I began to tidy up, as if it was a party that had just finished, rather than a life. I collected dirty crocks from round the living room and the kitchen and washed them up. I picked up and folded the clothes that had been hung on a rack to dry, and were long since dry. Some of these were Alicia's, rather than Bella's, but I placed them on the pile in the order I picked them up, not separating the clothing of the living from that of the dead, as if their two lives would forever be layered and interleaved. Then I rounded up the books from the sofa and the floor and the kitchen table and put them back in the bookcase. Some of these were in Italian, Alicia's first language, but most were books Bella had been reading. I knew this because we had discussed the books I was restoring to the shelf in the last days of her life.

When I had finished in the kitchen and the living room – wiped down the surfaces, plumped the cushions – I went into the bedroom. Alicia seemed to have fallen asleep so I tiptoed round the bed, bending over to pick up armfuls of clothes. As I straightened up with my bundle, I found Alicia's eyes were open and she was watching me, silently, and at the same time, I noticed there was a book, face down, beside the bed, where a hand reaching out from under the cover would fall on it. It was *The Bog People* by P. V. Glob. In a moment I was undone. I let fall the pile of clothes and, as Alicia had done in the car park, I sank to the ground and began to sob.

I became aware that Alicia was sitting beside me, patting my hand and murmuring to me in Italian. In her other hand she was holding against her cheek a purple embroidered jacket that Bella used to wear all the time, whether it went with the rest of her outfit or not. We sat on the floor until it grew dark, the book and the jacket sandwiched between us as we comforted each other with our memories. The next day, I wrote the first letter you answered. I hope you had someone to sit beside you, as you held the bracelet; someone to talk to about Birgitt.

I thought mostly of you, as I read your wife's story, how it must have felt for you. I never knew her, and I begin to feel I do know you. When I think of what it was like for you, left alone on the ferry, I wonder if I am being self-indulgent, letting myself go and wailing about whether my life has been worthwhile when I am, after all, still alive. Your loss is so much greater than any I have experienced, so abrupt and yet foreshadowed. As if Birgitt had been dying for years but it was never possible to admit she was, and there was never a moment when it became inevitable that she would. Until she did. Both the relationship and the manner of parting were so much more intense, in your case, than in mine. I regret having rattled on about Bella's death, now. I need never mention her again.

My final thought on this is: whatever else you have done or failed to have done, have experienced or missed experiencing, you have had that relationship with Birgitt. Something particular to you two, a closer, deeper relationship than many of us have a chance of knowing. I'm sorry you lost her. I'm pleased, for your sake, that she lived and you met her.

Thank you for telling me her story.

Tina

Silkeborg
22nd May

Dear Tina,

As I write this to you, I have the contents of my briefcase on the desk in front of me. That is: my laptop, my phone, my lunch, the *Copenhagen Post*, and your letter. Before Birgitt died, these things, except your letter, would have been, every day, in my briefcase, but there would also have been something she had put there, different each day. It might have been a drawing she had done, or something she had read and copied out for me, or the recipe for whatever we would be having for dinner. If she had no energy for such things, she would put an earring in my briefcase, or a glove, or a photo. Whatever it was, I understood it meant she was still alive and intended to be alive at the time I came home.

When I returned to work after her death, I carried my laptop and my phone and my paper and my lunch in my pockets or under my arm, so I would not have to open my briefcase and see, again and again, that there was nothing there but these things. Of course, this was at first, when I could not manage my grief. Now I can carry my briefcase with me and I do, every day. But each day it is a sadness for me to remember, as I open it, that it contains nothing to make me feel hopeful. I have never hoped for anything much. It was enough to know that Birgitt would be there when I returned home. Now I only hope for a return to hope, or at least to the feeling I once had that there is satisfaction in the little things of life.

It was two days after our thirtieth wedding anniversary when she died, twenty months ago. In all that time there has been nothing in my briefcase except tools for work, food and news about people I do not know and will never meet. Today, there is your letter.

Thank you.

Anders

Bury St Edmunds
1st June

Dear Anders,

I have never owned a briefcase. Or carried my lunch with me from home to a place of work, unless you count taking sandwiches out to the fields on occasion, during the harvest. I do, however, own a laptop.

Looking back at your letter of early May, I see you suggested we could continue our correspondence on a more joyous note, once you had told me the story of your wife. Instead, we seem to have become quite tearful. I may as well admit that your last letter made me cry. If I were to think of something it might comfort you to find in your briefcase, I will send it to you, as if it had fallen into the envelope when I wasn't looking. Although having had this lovely thought, I should probably not have shared it, so it would come as an unexpected bonus. There again, I may never find the right thing to send, and if I did, you might not recognise it as anything other than a piece of flotsam swept off the table as I wrote. You see how I am talking to you as if you were standing beside me?)

I am now going to proceed with some joyous news. My daughter, Mary, my youngest child, was married last week. We went to the church in the village, all dressed up, and Mary was escorted down the aisle, looking quite magnificent in a plain but elegant dress, by her father, looking as if he had been trussed up like one of his own hay bales in a hired morning suit. She married a young man called Vassily from Lithuania, whom she met when he came to work on some outbuildings we were converting into holiday cottages. He also had a hired morning suit and managed to look like a Bohemian prince come to claim his bride. After the ceremony we went to a hotel and there was food (which I did not cook and therefore enjoyed) and speeches. This went on all afternoon as the food was slow to arrive and the speeches had to be given, and then given again in the other language. After this, all the members of my family, except Mary and me, drank far more than they are used to or than is good for them. The Lithuanians drank considerably more than my family but were better at it. They travelled from sombre to gloriously cheerful, while I'm afraid many of our side of the room went from cheerful to maudlin or argumentative. Nevertheless, it was a pleasure for me to see Mary looking so happy.

I never expected her to marry. I'm not, you understand, suggesting that a woman's life is only fulfilled if she is a wife – I would have been happy for Mary to remain single – but we all need someone who is close; someone we care for and who cares for us, and up until she met Vassily, she did not appear to have any particular friends. She is a mystery to me, but so are all of my three children. I was all right when they were young and helpless and needed loving and nurturing. Edward was no good at this side of things but it came naturally to me and I was happy to cuddle and soothe and play. As soon as they reached an age where they had some self-determination, I had no idea how to behave towards them. They were so distinctly themselves and I didn't feel as if I had the right to tell them what to do, or even to give them advice. I had never made any choices for myself, or not the right ones, so who was I to guide them? Edward was much better at this stage of their lives. I would say he took them by the hand and led them to the places they have ended up, but it was a rather more brutal (not in any physical sense) process than that. He was confident he knew what was the best path for them and he gave them no choice, though they seemed not to want one, and lo and behold, he was right. They have all ended up, in one way or another, working on the farm, and they seem to want to be doing it.

My two boys, Tam and Andrew, have turned into farmers without ever looking to right or left at the other choices they might have made. Mary qualified as an accountant and then came home to do the books. The women of my acquaintance congratulate me on having pulled off the trick of keeping my children together in the place where they were brought up, forever around to delight me and make me feel anchored. Although I say 'congratulate', I know, and they know, that it is nothing to do with me; they are commenting on what they see as my undeserved good luck.

Mary is more than just the farm's bookkeeper. She does the accounts for many of the farmers and agricultural businesses in the area. She is also the one with all the ideas on how to improve our farm's income. Not just the reduction of input costs and the maximisation of high-value outputs, which is what Edward, Tam and Andrew talk about all the time – less fertiliser, less manpower, higher-yield crops. Mary is the one who finds grants for replacing hedges, maintaining field margins, managing water courses. If it were not for her, we would not be making money by generating electricity through solar panels. And we would not be providing tourist accommodation, which is how Vassily came into our lives.

I thought Mary would never be close to anyone because she seemed to care so little for what anyone thought of her. She is extremely forthright; she does not say much and what she does say is not about opinions or emotions, but facts. When someone else says something stupid or, in her view, wrong, she says so. I sometimes think English is a language with too many options on how to express a single thought, and we tend to use this to the full, in conversation, wrapping up a criticism in phrases that reduce its impact. Mary never does this. She is lean and tall and strong-featured, like her mother, and has always been, I fear, easier to dislike than to like. Vassily also speaks very rarely, and not just because his English is limited. With his Lithuanian friends he is the silent one. I wondered at first if Mary liked him for not expressing opinions she disagreed with; I had no idea why he liked her. However, they are suited to each other, and as I watched them at the reception, I knew they would be happy. Something about the way they turned their heads towards each other without speaking, or touched each other without forethought or purpose.

So Mary is happy. Edward is happy, because she has secured building skills for the benefit of the family business. I am happy because I love my daughter and want her to be happy but have had no idea how to bring this about since she stopped wanting me to play with her. Now that burden has been taken away from me by Vassily.

A joyful outcome. Tell me about your children.

Best wishes,

Tina

Silkeborg
12th June

My dear Tina,

Thank you for your joyful letter, and for the feather, which I know did not fall from the table as you wrote but was chosen by you, for me. You know I deal in objects and the first step in understanding an object is to be able to name it. To give it a category. I am enjoying the feather, when I open my briefcase, but really, I need to know: what bird is this from? What part of the bird? I could look through books identifying birds, or even on the internet, and at last I expect I would match my feather to a species, but you are closer to birds, with the life you lead, and I am sure you can tell me what I want to know. I would rather you told me.

As you tell me you have a laptop, I wonder if you wanted to continue this correspondence by electronic means? I have thought carefully before I suggested this. I may as well confess, now, that when your first letter to Professor Glob arrived and I picked it up to reply, I was irritated you had not included an e-mail address. If you had, I would have replied at once by e-mail. I would have written something like: 'I am afraid Professor Glob is no longer with us. If you wish to visit the museum, please see the website,' and I would have copied and pasted the link and clicked on 'send'. I have found that it is no use to write an e-mail longer than three or four lines, because whoever receives it will not read to the end.

Instead, I had to compose a letter. I could picture you reading the letter and I imagined you would do this slowly and carefully, so I felt I needed to write my letter to you slowly and carefully. I had to be sure I had read yours to Professor Glob slowly and carefully so that I could be sure to address the points you made. So we have gone on. We have written at length and thoughtfully, and to do this, we have both had to read the letters we received in a thoughtful way. The writing and the reading have both been such an unexpected pleasure to me, I would like to be sure we will not lose this – that is, the length and the thoughtfulness. However, I am so used to communicating by computer, I find the business of sending letters an awkward interruption of the conversation we are having – finding the envelope, the stamp, visiting the post box, waiting for days before I can be sure you have read what I have written, when I want my thoughts to reach you as they occur to me.

So I have a proposal. Instead of the envelope and the stamp, we could attach our letters to an e-mail. I will do this only if I can be sure you will treat them as carefully as you have treated the letters sent by post. I would like to think you will print them out; save them up to be read, slowly and carefully, when you have time, instead of clicking on the attachment and scrolling down the screen as soon as the e-mail catches your eye. Will you do this? It would make me feel more in touch with you. If you say no, I will, of course, carry on with the envelopes and the stamps. I would cycle miles in the rain, if I had to (which I don't), to post letters to you, if this was the only way to make sure you continued to write to me. And you must go on with the envelopes and the stamps, if that is what you would prefer, for your letters to me.

You ask about my children. I have a daughter, Karin, and a son, Erik. They are a marvel to me. When they were growing up I was so much occupied with keeping Birgitt happy I never really thought of them as separate people, just as members of this family forever working to hold itself together. It was our job, as a family, to keep Birgitt happy. I do not remember being anxious about them, as most parents, I believe, are anxious. Only after Birgitt had gone, and we were grieving together, did I think about them as adults, with their own lives to lead.

When Birgitt was alive and the children were young, we went often to the island where Birgitt's grandparents lived.

The house is still there and we still own it. We came to know the other families who visited each summer, for this is a place of summer visitors, now. It would have been a bleak and isolated place to live. I did not enjoy those holidays very much. Each time Birgitt walked away from us, towards the sea or along the sands, I feared she would never turn back. I used to watch her so hard my eyes would start to see things that weren't there; I would mistake a rock for a boat or a bush for a person, and so often, after she had turned and was walking towards us, I was sure I could still see her, walking away. Where other fathers would be watching their children, worrying if they were safe and happy, I was watching my wife. The children always were safe; they were sensible, well-behaved children, and if Birgitt kept walking until she would in a moment or two be out of sight, it was often one of them, or both of them, who ran after her to remind her it was late, or cold, or suppertime, while I was still trying to work out what was reflection or shadow and what was my wife in the midst of the sea and the sand. (What was? What were? You must correct me if I go wrong).

After she left us, we went back, the three of us, and now that I had only them to watch, it felt as if I was noticing them for the first time, and it amazed me to see how self-possessed they were. We were in the deepest grief and talked to each other all the time, mostly about Birgitt and their childhood. I do not usually talk much. I find I do not often have anything to say which it would interest other people to hear. Though other people talk about things I am not interested in and I am happy to listen, so maybe it is not others' lack of the will to listen but my lack of interest in speaking that is at fault. As we talked, the children and I, I could see that even in their grief,

Karin and Erik were perfectly in control, capable of managing themselves. I don't know how this happened. It had little enough to do with me. When you talked of your daughter Mary, you said you had been at a loss to know how to make her happy. I am ashamed to say I don't remember ever having understood it was my job to make my children happy.

Karin is a lawyer working in Copenhagen and Erik is an architect in Stockholm. They made such sensible but hard career choices. Both of them had to study for a long time, and faced much competition in order to do what they wanted to do. Both their professions, I feel, require understanding, empathy and some measure of creativity. I am very proud of them both. I do not see them as often as I would like, though they are both diligent in visiting me or inviting me to visit them. Karin has phoned to say she will come and stay next month. I am looking forward to it.

Write soon. Do not forget about the feather.

Best wishes,

Anders

Bury St Edmunds
16th June

Dear Anders,

I am sending this, as you suggest, as an attachment to an e-mail. I have loved the method we used to talk to each other; the physical effort involved in finding the paper, the envelope, the stamps, the time to go to the post box, and the time delay before I receive a reply. All this makes our letters seem so much more important than a few lines of text on a screen.

Most of the e-mails I receive are about special offers on plants, or notification of farming events, or reminders that it is my turn to run the Women's Institute cake stall at the farmers' market. Your letters are a world apart from all that. I feel I know what it must have been like to be the last generation for whom gaslight or candlelight was normal, and electricity the new invention. I am looking back over my shoulder, writing letters, knowing the new way of communicating is more efficient but wanting to hold on to the softness and elegance we are leaving behind. Mostly, though, I want us to stay in touch, and so this is an attachment, sent electronically. I promise, if you reply the same way, that I will print out what you send and read it as if it had arrived through the door, in an envelope. Will you make me the same promise? To read as carefully and to think as carefully about a reply before sending it? Of course, if I find something else I want to send, like the bird's feather, I will do that by post.

It is the wing feather from a female pheasant. I am teetering, here, between telling you everything I know about pheasants, as if you know nothing, and simply letting that first sentence stand, as if it told you everything you needed to know about the feather I sent you. I am hesitating to tell you everything I know, not only because I do not want to presume you know nothing, but also because I might sound as if I am trying to prove that I, like you, know some facts. I might sound as if I was trumping your information on Iron Age life with my information on game birds. It is not at all likely I would do that because I am woefully devoid of ambition to prove myself better than someone else, and always have been. When someone does something well, I might wish I could do it just as well. But I have never felt I needed to strive to do it better. It is a fault, I think. I ought to have had a better idea of myself.

I will tell you about pheasants, and just hope it is not too boring. We have breeding pens on our land; a local shoot manages the birds and half a dozen times a year a convoy of 4x4 vehicles and a trailer or two turn up full of men all wearing caps and carrying guns. Several pick-ups arrive with men, boys and the occasional woman in the back, carrying sticks with pieces of white plastic feed sack tied to them. They climb out and set off over the fields waving their sticks to drive the pheasants up off the ground into the air. The 'guns', as they are known, as if all humanity had left them for the purposes of this sport, go and stand by markers and shoot the bewildered pheasants, who only yesterday were being fed by some of those now trying to kill them, as they fly over wondering what on earth is going on. (I am being anthropomorphic – pheasants are an exceptionally stupid bird and doubtless have no thoughts in their heads at all.) Muddy, excited but obedient dogs collect the carcasses, which are strung up in rows on a sort of scaffolding set up in one of the trailers for the purpose. In the middle of the day, the beaters and the guns find a shelter or, in the unlikely event that the weather is fine enough, a bank where they sit and eat the sandwiches their wives have prepared. At the end of the day they carry off their share of the dead birds and their muddy dogs in their 4x4s and go home to their wives. Edward and Tam are among those designated as guns on these days, and so I know from experience that the wives are expected to congratulate the returning warrior, hang up the spoils somewhere convenient and then clean up the mud carried into the kitchen by the dog and the gun. Later, when the birds are almost, but not quite, too rotten to eat, the grateful wife will pluck and draw them and put them in the freezer. The number of pheasants in the freezer is kept at a constant level by serving up pheasant, on occasion, but mainly by the surreptitious disposal of birds not yet eaten, as newer trophies arrive.

I know I sound scornful, but actually I am ambivalent about this pastime. On the one hand, it is ridiculous behaviour, breeding and feeding birds, persuading them to fly and then shooting them. If the flesh of the birds was highly prized and the flavour was enhanced by terrifying them before blasting them out of the sky – rather than just wringing their necks like a chicken – it would be less absurd. In fact, no one that I know chooses to eat pheasant very often, or at all, and the most ardent fan of shooting does not claim the meat tastes better. On the other hand, the shoot requires copses, hedgerows, strips of field planted with otherwise unproductive crops like sunflowers, and if they were banned, or ceased to operate, there would be no need for this much diversity and parts of the countryside I value would be turned into arable land. Also, I like the pheasants and the dogs. The pheasants, as I have said, are brainless, but they have a trick of hiding in a bush or clump of grass and breaking cover, when disturbed, with the most wonderful clatter of alarm, and gliding off over the nearest open space like a perfectly formed paper aeroplane. They are pretty, too. The males are (I'm sure you know this) the more colourful, but the females' feathers have the beauty of a symmetrical pattern in shades of brown and cream, without any showiness. I like patterns more than colours. Have you ever looked at the frond of a fern as it unfurls? It is a masterpiece of complexity without a single random element. I like dogs because there is no artifice in a dog. They can be cunning and underhand but only in a predictable way.

I enjoy the enjoyment Tam and Edward have from the sport, if it can be called such. They are sober, hard-working men and it pleases me to see them excited, insofar as they are capable of excitement, as they set off, and to hear the contentment in their conversation afterwards, about the day they have spent. It is, after all, a ritual, and ritual gives a pattern to the season. Edward and Tam would reject this view, of course. If asked to justify the shooting of pheasants they would cite the economics (the shoot pays us money) and countryside management (the shoot controls predators) and social cohesion (it keeps men and boys off the streets and out in the fresh air). They would be reluctant to admit they do it because they enjoy it and that that alone might be justification enough.

I should point out that the feather I sent was not from a bird killed by the shoot. All that is over for the summer and the birds are wandering about, the survivors, pairing up and searching for food like ordinary birds do. I took the feather from a female hit by a car on the lane leading to our farm. I'm pleased you like it. Knowing this one feather is important to you will make all the other, similar feathers I see lying about more important to me.

Yesterday, when I was picking some early raspberries, I was thinking about the way the Iron Age people expected to experience another life, after the one they were living. Whenever I pick raspberries, I go as carefully as possible down the row, looking for every ripe fruit. But however careful I am, when I turn round to go back the other way, I find fruit I had not seen approaching the plants from the opposite direction. Another life, I thought, might be like a second pass down the row of raspberry canes; there would be good things I had not come across in my first life, but I suspect I would find much of the fruit was already in my basket. You see, I am being much more sanguine since I first wrote to you, when Bella had just died. When we started this correspondence, I thought I would gain more from putting my thoughts in writing than I would in receiving your replies. But I was wrong. Your letters have become important to me. Do not worry about your English. It is perfect.

Write soon.

Warmest wishes,

Tina

Silkeborg
23rd June

Dear Tina,

I printed out your last letter, which, like all the rest, is important to me, and read it, as you asked, as if it had arrived in an envelope. Already, I feel more connected to you, by seeing your name in my inbox. But please send by post anything you would like me to see, and touch. That, too, is special.

I have never picked raspberries, but I understand the point you are making. Unlike you, I feel I have overlooked far too many of the fruits in this life I have. Always looking down, as it were, at what is close to me, rather than at the top and bottom of the bush, in amongst the leaves. I have more reason than you to hope for another life when I would have the chance to find some of the harvest I have missed. (Now I wonder if the word 'fruit' can be plural, but I will not interrupt myself while I am writing to you to look it up.)

I think you are right to be tolerant of people who kill pheasants in the name of sport. It is, as you say, a ritual. In the same way the Tollund Man was killed, as a ritual. In his case, though, the ritual was part of acting out a myth, a story invented by men (and women, of course; I am using 'men' to stand for 'mankind') to try to understand themselves and their world. The Tollund Man's contemporaries made sense of life and avoided being terrified of death by inventing alternative, mythical worlds where the gods acted out dramas that affected the human condition by, for example, influencing the seasons and the fertility of the soil. Just telling a story is not the same as believing it, and believing it is not the same as acting it out. I am saying (with too many words as usual) that ritual is a very important part of believing in a myth and that myths are very important for giving comfort and making sense of the world.

You may say you did not mean 'ritual' in quite the way I am using the word when you referred to your husband and son shooting pheasants, but it seems to me that part of the story they tell themselves about who they are is to do with the provision of food. Standing in the cold and the rain without any certainty of acquiring food, with the chance of escape for the pheasant and failure for them, is a way of acting out the purpose of their lives, as it were, at the extreme. As the death of the Tollund Man may have been seen by the whole community as acting out their own eventual deaths through the death of one man. We have an instinct for violence that has the approval of authority, and shooting a few birds is a better way of indulging in this than the alternatives – war, executions, human sacrifice.

I have had these thoughts about myth often, over the years,

because, of course, it was a myth that Birgitt had created in her own mind that governed her life. She saw the imagined world alongside the real one so clearly, and yearned to reach it, as I have said. It might have helped her to have had some rituals that brought them closer together, but she never worked out how to create the bridge, give herself a railing to hang on to. She had what other people would call odd habits, which did seem to give her comfort from time to time. I never used the word 'ritual' to describe these, for fear of appearing superstitious. Superstition is such a scornful word, applied by rational people to anything that appears not to be a rational belief, not seeing there is beauty and meaning and purpose in putting aside everything that can be explained and imagining something quite miraculous in, for example, an unfurling fern frond.

Back to Birgitt. One of her habits was picking things up. Stones, twigs, items left lying around in public places like pieces of ribbon or safety pins. It did not matter if these were beautiful or not, if they were natural or manufactured, something would tug at her eye and she would pick it up and put it in her pocket. Some of these things I would never see again but some of them I have still, in my house, sitting just where she put them, in the exact arrangement she put them in.

She was fierce and determined when she had seen something she wanted. It was hard to divert her or turn her back. We had some moments of embarrassment. In a shoe shop once, when the children were quite small, we were buying shoes for them for the new term about to start. We were sitting in a row on a bench waiting for the assistant to bring the shoes we had picked out in the right sizes for the children's feet. Erik saw a friend of his on another bench and got up and hopped over to him, one shoe on and one shoe off. Karin fell sideways to fill the space where he had been, feet still hanging down and kicking the front of the bench. Her hair became caught in the strap of my watch and I remember feeling helpless and hopeless. They were good children, I know, well-behaved, but yet it all seemed too much: that Erik should run off; that I could not go after him because of Karin's hair; that she would not sit up or stop kicking the bench, whatever I said. I think my mind was always on Birgitt, and so however small a distraction the children created, it was almost more than I could bear.

I untangled Karin's hair and went over to Erik, who was playing quietly with his friend. I knew the mother and spoke to her for a few minutes and when I looked round, Karin had her feet up on the bench and was lying back with her knees in the air, holding the hem of her skirt above her head. Birgitt was gone. My first thought was to rush to the shop doorway as if my wife was a child not to be trusted outside on the street, but I heard her voice and found her behind a rack of shoes. She was holding a shoelace. It was long and striped, diagonally, in gold and green. It was new and the woman she was talking to had obviously been explaining that it needed to go back into the box she was holding in her hand, with a pair of new shoes in it, only one of them with laces. Birgitt was telling her the lace was not meant to be shut up in a box. It wouldn't be, the woman explained, when someone bought the shoes. She was calm and pleasant. I asked Birgitt if she wanted to buy the shoes, and she said no, of course not. Then I asked the woman if she could sell us a pair of the same laces. Unfortunately not, she said. They were only available with the shoes.

'It was just lying there,' Birgitt said to me, 'spare.'

'You can't have it, though,' I said. 'It isn't spare.'

'I know,' she said.

Later I asked what it was about the lace that had made her want it. The continuous pattern of it, she said, the shape-making properties.

Another time we were on a train and she became fascinated by a wisp of sea-green scarf a woman sitting near us was wearing round her neck. I knew what Birgitt was looking at because it was often things such as this scarf and the lace that attracted her – things that moved in the breeze, in odd colours, not solid or bulky but long and able to be re-formed into different shapes. We neither of us spoke of it but when the woman stood up to leave the train, Birgitt followed her out of the carriage and came back a little later looking sorrowful.

'She wouldn't let me have it,' she said.

None of the things I have left of Birgitt's is like the scarf and the shoelace. What she kept tended to be more solid, and I wonder if she was seeking something that tied one thing to another, and never finding it. The wisp of material or length of string that would have made a connection between her two forms of reality always eluded her.

I am making her sound childlike, in the way she reached out for things that were not hers to take, and I suppose she was. But meek, where a child would be passionate.

I will end with another thought about shooting pheasants: it means a close relationship with nature. I am so far detached from nature in my habits. I have only two hobbies – playing chess and singing in a choir – and both take place indoors.

My only exercise is swimming (in an indoor pool) and cycling to work. Since we have started this correspondence, I have paid more attention as I cycle. To reach the centre of Silkeborg, where the museum is, I have to cross a lake. I notice the water, because it changes all the time and reflects the day; the colour is grey on dull days, more blue on bright days; the surface is ruffled by the wind or (not often) quite still. But now I am reminding myself to look at the scenery too, not to cycle with my head down, watching the road and the lake. There are woods around Silkeborg, and an old towpath alongside the river Gudenå. I think: I must go for a walk. Look for unfurling fern fronds. In the pursuit of a more joyful outlook.

    With all my good wishes,

    Anders

Bury St Edmunds
1st July

Dear Anders,

I like the way you talk of what is so often spoken of as if it was simple, like ritual, and give it depth and meaning. Everything we do on the farm has a flavour of ritual about it. When the crops are sown, when the animals are mated, when the young are slaughtered. There is no superstition in this; there are practical, rational reasons for doing what we do – but we make it into a ritual with all the little ceremonies that surround it. Once, I was in Italy visiting Bella when harvesting of our main cereal crops started. I had forgotten to make, and leave behind, the fruitcake it is a tradition (there's another word for ritual) in our family to eat on that particular day. The weather that year became unpredictable after the harvest began. It rained at the wrong time. As well as reducing the yield, it meant the dryer in one of the barns was running, day after day, to bring down the moisture content of the grain, an audible reminder that all was not perfect. Edward said, making a joke of it, that the lack of the fruitcake was the cause of all this. An ill omen bringing misfortune.

The whole business of farming does sometimes seem like a fight there is a chance we will not win, and the closer to losing we are, the more hard, physical effort involved in pulling us back from the brink, the happier everyone is. Except me. I enjoy being warm, dry and idle following an afternoon battling sheets of plastic over a silage clamp in a snowstorm, but I don't feel any sort of satisfaction at having tethered the sheet, saved the silage. Although I spend so much of my time in the kitchen, putting food on the table, providing food is not part of the story I tell myself of my life. I think the only myth I have to sustain me is the idea of the Tollund Man. He is, to me, like the gods he believed in; someone who lived before me and fought battles and now has wisdom he could impart to me if I could find a way to reach him. The constant planning to go and never going – that is maybe taking the place of a ritual. But thinking of it like that makes a decision to go seem even more significant, even more a step into something big, so I will not follow the thought through for fear of making it seem too great ever to be taken. I do still plan to come. It is still important to me to take this step; though Bella will not be with me, I know you would be there to greet me as I walked into the museum. But I do not feel I can say that tomorrow or next month or even next year is when this should happen. I am hoping I will know when it is the right time.

Warmest wishes,
Tina

Silkeborg
10th July

Dear Tina,

I am looking forward to standing beside you when you meet the Tollund Man for the first time. I hope it is soon, but I trust you to know when the time has come.

I had a visit from my daughter, and I will tell you about it because it was a joyful occasion, though the joy was hidden inside it and I am finding it out now she has gone back to Copenhagen. I am hoping to find it out by writing to you. I fear this will be a long letter.

Karin arrived on Friday evening, with food. I treat food carefully, in my solitary life. Every evening I prepare what I am going to eat, I put out a mat and knife and fork and the glass for beer or wine or water, the pepper and the salt. I take the plate with the food I have cooked and sit at the table to eat it. Then I clear everything up and leave the kitchen as it was before I started. I do this because it is a version of the custom we followed when Birgitt was alive. Following this same pattern has felt important to me to keep the surface of my life from tilting and tipping me into a form of shameful despair. I am no cook, though. I eat sausages and potatoes, or chops and potatoes, or ham with salad and bread. I do not enjoy the food, not the preparation of it nor the eating of it. I know I need it, that is all.

Karin is an adventurous cook. She lives, as I said, in Copenhagen, where there is a new culture of seasonal food, and food collected from the wild, which I do not understand. I cannot tell you what she cooked for me because I am not sure of the Danish words for the ingredients or the type of dish so I have no idea what the English words would be. I should have asked for details, written it down for you. I only thought of this later. At the time I was enjoying watching her doing the preparation and the cooking and the sort of conversation you have, when one of you is occupied and the other is idle. We spoke of television programmes we had watched, recent events. I am worried about the changes taking place in the world, but she is not. She is young enough to be relaxed about change. She knows she has a lifetime ahead of her and she might regret the decisions some of the people or the politicians are taking and think it may mean there will be economic or social troubles, but, still, there is time for things to improve again before she is old. Perhaps this has nothing to do with age, but is just because she is an optimistic person with a hopeful outlook on life.

The food was delicious. Rich and earthy. As we ate it I told her about your pheasant shoot. Wasn't that, I said, the sort of food she liked? Seasonal. Foraged. She was not so sure. There is a difference, she said, between harvesting a naturally occurring abundance and creating an abundance in order to harvest it – which is, of course, farming.

'If I was in court,' she said, summing up, 'I would prefer to be putting the case for pheasant shooting to be classified as a form of farming, rather than defending it as a form of foraging.'

When we had the kitchen tidy and clean we went outside

to sit in the summerhouse I have in the garden and she told me what she had come to say. It was dusk and there are no lights outside so I could see her only dimly; she could see me only dimly and I think this was for the better. You said to me, in your first letter – the first one that was addressed to me rather than the first letter you wrote, to Professor Glob – that you were writing for yourself and I need not bother to read on. I am going to do the same thing now. I am going to write down the story Karin told me to help me decide what I feel about it. I am not going to say you need not bother to read it because I know you well enough now to know you will. Also, I want you to read it because your opinion on it will help me to know you better still.

For the last two years Karin has had a partner called Lars, a man involved in various ways in the music industry – the pop music industry, that is. I have never understood exactly what he does because I do not understand how the industry works, but I believe he manages bands and is a disc jockey and maybe has other ways of making money. It does not matter now because the first thing Karin had to tell me was that this relationship was over. I was not sorry. He is a big, untidy, cheerful man and so completely unlike me, which is often a reason for liking someone, but in this case, I thought it was a way he chose to present himself. I have no idea what sort of man he truly is, and I prefer people to be more direct. To be plain about what opinions they hold. I am afraid some of my distrust might have been because I am distrustful of the business he is in. I find it hard to judge the quality of modern music so am suspicious of it. Of course, it is not up to me to make this judgement. It is only up to me to decide if I like to listen to it, or not, and if I do, the quality is as high as I need it to be. History will decide if I was right in the choices I made.

Now Karin tells me it is over; she knew he was a man of large appetites, she said, and that he enjoyed satisfying them, but something had happened to make her realise there were no boundaries when she had thought boundaries existed. Here is what happened.

Within Copenhagen there is an area called Christiania, which is a sort of commune, with a licence to break the law. There are entertainments available there that the police do not bother to inquire into unless there is a disturbance, if someone is actually hurt, and even then, so I understand, the authorities are reluctant to enter. I have never been there. I do not disapprove at all; I believe it is a good thing for there to be such places where people bolder than I am can indulge themselves without harming others. It is somewhere Lars went, often, and Karin went with him. One night, about three or four months ago, they went to a bar in Christiania where Lars had arranged to meet some friends. The friends were not there and had not arrived when Lars looked at his phone and told Karin he had to go. There was a deal he was trying to do with a band and they were also in Christiania that night, at another bar, and it was important he spoke to them. He would not be long, he said, and she could wait where she was for the friends to arrive.

Karin is a strong person but she became uneasy, sitting in the bar alone. She rang Lars, but his phone was switched off. So she stood up and left the bar, which was not easy to achieve as the crowd had become thicker, and more lively. She felt hands holding her back although, she says, she may only have imagined this. She was trying not to allow herself to be afraid.

Out in the street, she turned to the left, having a feeling Lars had turned to the left, and set out to look for him, walking close to the buildings and looking into the bars and food stalls and at the people sitting out on the pavements.

Three men coming the other way jostled against her, then paused and spoke to her, and she found she could not interpret their mood; were they mocking or teasing, were they menacing or, as their words suggested, merely being polite, trying to apologise. She looked squarely at them and, without speaking or smiling, went to step round them, but they shifted and her way was blocked. Above the smells of fried food and the smoke of a hundred joints, she smelt sweat, old leather and the tang of motor oil from the jacket of the man nearest to her.

People were passing by, one or two glancing in their direction, conscious of some uncertainty in the behaviour of those forming the group she was unwillingly part of: something which might or might not develop. As Karin moved again, still trying to deny the knowledge that these strangers were, in truth, preventing her from going forward, one of the passersby stopped and spoke her name. He was a man she had met just a few times, at parties, or as one of a group having a drink or a meal. All she knew about him was his nationality – Australian – and his occupation – journalist. She could not remember his name. But she greeted him as if he was an old friend, the very friend she had been walking down this street to meet, and the next moment, the men around her had gone, were already weaving away and turning the corner, careless and cheerful.

The Australian, whose name, he reminded her, was Ben, asked if she was alone and when she said yes, he waved on the party he was with and stayed with her. He had not seen Lars, but he had seen a flyer advertising an appearance by the band Lars had said he was going to find, and he remembered the venue. They were now in the area where stalls openly sell hash and there were young people and not-so-young people sway-ing on their feet or lying down on the road. Ben put an arm round Karin's shoulder and steered her through the crowd. He was quite a big man, and sober, and he had no difficulty finding a way through. Now she was no longer alone, Karin also felt more sure of herself – more herself, you might say – and strode forward with her usual sense of entitlement and fearlessness in a public place.

When they reached the venue, an old brick warehouse, it was obvious the concert had finished. The doors were wide open and the lights inside had been turned up full. On the stage, the band's amplifiers and instruments were being unplugged and packed up. Karin recognised one of the band members and called out to him. He raised his head and stopped, perfectly still. He looked wary. He spoke to the other people working on the stage, quickly, in a low voice, and they all came to a standstill, turned towards her, leads, speakers, guitars, microphones in their hands. In the silence, Karin caught the sound of laughter from a doorway beside the stage, and she sprinted towards it and into a cubicle where the performers changed their clothes. Lars was there. He was stretched out, half undressed, on an old sofa beside the lead vocalist, a girl with almost no clothes on who was nibbling Lars's ear.

Lars lifted his head to look at Karin, then let it fall back on the cushions. He took a pull at the joint he held in the hand that was not holding the lead vocalist's body tight to his, and offered it to her. The infidelity did not surprise her; it was not even serious. His attraction to the lead vocalist was unlikely to be more than physical; she doubted he would remember her name in a month's time. The boundary Lars had crossed was leaving Karin alone, and vulnerable – because however much she tried to be strong she had felt vulnerable. She had believed that he was prepared to stray only if it was not at her cost.

She walked out into the hall, where clearing up had begun again. The band and their helpers were tossing lines of song back and forth as they worked, punctuated with a chord struck on a guitar or a note held on a keyboard. She walked quickly to the open doors and out into the chill dark night. When she was in the shadows, clear of the light falling from the concert hall windows, she sat down on a block of concrete decorated in a pink and blue and orange pattern with slogans declaring defiance to authority. She sat down on it and put her head in her hands, angry, disgusted and ashamed, with Lars, with herself. When she looked up, Ben was leaning on a railing beside her.

'I thought you might need company on the way home,' he said.

All this is not really the point of the story Karin told me. It is, I suppose, an ordinary enough story. It is an explanation, though, of what happened next; justification, perhaps. You may judge for yourself. She told me all this, in this much detail, so I could judge for myself about what happened next.

She went home with Ben. Not to her home, which she shared with Lars, but to the apartment Ben was renting in Christianshavn, the suburb of which Christiania is a part. She stayed there for five days and five nights. She abandoned

herself, was the way she described it to me. A release from
the tension, a way of dismissing the anger and hurt. It is
not the way she would normally behave. She is a cool girl.
I think the word 'cool' has another meaning than the one I
mean it to stand for here. I mean she is not easily made hot.
When she gives way to passion, it is as a result of having
understood the consequences. A considered decision to let go.

She went out and bought clothes and walked to work and
ignored phone calls from Lars and walked back to Ben's apartment. On the seventh day, Ben flew back to Australia. Karin
did not go to see him off at the airport. She kissed him good-
bye like she would kiss a friend who has been good to her but
who is not going to be important to her in the future. That is
how she described her feelings, on the steps of the apartment
block, as he climbed into a taxi.

Then she went home to the apartment she lives in, and
which she owns, and told Lars to leave. I have spoken to her
many times on the phone since then, and she has always
sounded happy. I have not had reasons to be fearful about
her. Sitting in my shed, in the dark, she still sounded happy
as she told me she is pregnant. She did not mean to conceive,
however, and it was a shock to her. There is no possibility this
is Lars's child. She has known for three months, now, but the
news was, of course, new to me and my first thought was a
joyous one. A baby. There is nothing more joyous than that.
But no sooner had I felt this happiness than I was overcome
with despair. What would happen now, to my lovely Karin?
Would she pack herself up and go to Australia to join the
baby's father, a man I had never met and might dislike or
distrust? Or would she be left alone to raise the child, with no
one to share the responsibility with? Was there, I wondered,

a way for her to do the job she does in Copenhagen here in Silkeborg, so I could be the person who carried the burden with her? Would she come to me, or should I retire early and go to her, to Copenhagen? The first thing I said, through the turmoil of these thoughts, was: 'Have you decided not to have an abortion?'

This was a cruel thing to say, implying I thought this was the best solution when, if she had said she was still considering the option, I would have been as upset for the child I would never meet as if he or she was already sitting in my arms and was about to be taken from me. In fact, she said:

'I have decided that. I will have the baby.'

She had, of course, thought it all through. Coolly. The baby has been given to her, as she sees it, as it might be through sperm donation. The week with Ben was like a story she told herself. The baby is the happy ending. She has heard from Ben once since he left, to let her know he had arrived home and to say thank you for a wonderful few days. She did not reply and does not intend to reply. She will not tell him she is pregnant. When she says this, I am truly shocked. Has he not the right to know? I ask. She says: For generations women had no rights except those granted them by men. Now, if a woman claims the right to deny a man something he believes he is entitled to, why should this be so shocking? Is it not the way it has always been, only with the genders reversed? She is denying him nothing he has asked for or expects. She is asking for and expecting nothing from him. It is, she repeats, like sperm donation.

Early next morning, she left to return to Copenhagen and I was still not sure what I felt about the story she had told me. I had said so little. I said, of course, that whatever she decided to do I would help her in any way I was able. She said: 'I have decided.' She looked at me with defiance, for just a moment, then she smiled and kissed me. She does not need to be defiant with me. I am not going to challenge her; that is for other people.

But what do you think? Should I argue with her about the rights of the father? All the time she was telling me the story, in the gloomy little shed, I had in my mind the thought of writing to you. I listened better, I think, to be sure of telling you the story without any errors. I hope I have done that. Whether you feel you can tell me your opinion, if you have an opinion, is less important than the comfort it has given me to be able to share all this. I would never have believed it could be so.

Thank you.
Anders

Bury St Edmunds
20th July

My dear Anders,
I believe I have already told you that I do not often hold strong opinions; I am rarely confident of being in the right. I find it difficult not to see both sides of a story. This is a good thing, I think, and also a bad thing. I am not easily outraged, and outrage is so often a waste of energy. I find it easy to sympathise with those who appear to be the sinners as well as those who appear in the role of victim; I don't know if this makes me a better person than someone who condemns

without hesitation, but it does make me like myself a little better. On the other hand, I have tended to accept what someone else feels strongly is right, because I can so clearly see their point of view and I have not felt strongly enough about the alternative to stand by it. You could say that is why I married Edward. My parents and his parents were eloquent about the impact on them, the baby, Edward and me, if we did not marry each other. This was all so true, and so the fact that it was not what I had wanted to do with my life, that it was a short-term solution and that it put the immediate well-being of others ahead of my own long-term well-being – all of this seemed flimsy in comparison. I could not express it with any conviction.

My mother thought I was not so much able to see all sides as desperate to avoid conflict at all costs, which was entirely a product of my position in the family, as the middle child of three. She was a lovely woman, my mother, but fond of categories. (I know I am diverting away from the point of this letter, which is to respond to the story you told me, but I will do that, I promise.) I was irritated by the simplicity of my mother's view of the world, when I was younger, but now that I know how hard it is to keep upright, cheerful, balanced and in control, which is expected of us as adults, I can appreciate the mechanisms she used to achieve this. There was no subtlety and no malice in the judgements she made. Every family, according to her, would be either 'well off' or 'struggling'. I asked once which we were, and she was upset, which should have made me feel guilty but did not, at the time. The categories were there to keep a distance between herself and the people she saw as able to cope better than she could; a distance that prevented her being judged in her turn.

I am mentioning this because I don't know how much of my willingness to see everyone's point of view at the same time is because that is my nature, or whether by repeating the mantra so often my mother made me believe it, and therefore live up to it, and therefore allow it to become true. Or – here's an odd thought – she may have been right. I have three children and the middle one, Andrew, is the most thoughtful, the kindest, I think. But he has no difficulty in asserting his opinion, whereas I do.

I am not, in any event, the best person to ask for an opinion on the decisions your daughter has made. Except that I feel strongly she has a right to make her own decisions. But you will want to be certain she has not been entirely influenced by emotions that might turn out to be misleading her.

I have mentioned our correspondence to no one. It felt like a conversation with no room in it for others, like the best conversations with a close friend. However, you spoke of sharing our discussion on the pheasants with your daughter and this made me think I should share your daughter's story with my daughter. I wanted to have a point of view clearly expressed, as I know Mary, who is a very certain person and a plain speaker, would express it. Then, I thought, I would be able to see the other point of view, the alternative, clearly enough to be able, perhaps, to give you a strong opinion.

Mary and Vassily are living in a converted outbuilding on the other side of the yard. Vassily converted it himself as a holiday let, before he became part of the family. It is a very plain sort of building, inside and out. Fit for purpose, you might say; the conversion was carried out without spending money on anything a summer visitor would not need or would not miss. I thought, when Mary and Vassily moved in, they would make it less plain – put down rugs, hang up colour-ful curtains, paint the walls a colour that was not white, buy ornaments and pictures and extra pieces of furniture. Make it, in other words, more like the farmhouse where Edward and I live. We have geological deposits of belongings in every room on every surface; things we inherited from Edward's par-ents and grandparents, from mine, things given to us or (the smallest group, this) bought by us. Mary and Vassily, starting with the bedrock, so to speak, had a choice of how thick and diverse a stratum to lay on top – heaven knows, I was ready enough to shovel up some of the accumulation of things in my house for them to have. They have done nothing. Tam's wife, Sarah, who has made the interior of the bungalow we built for Edward's parents a nest of her own construction (I'm mixing my metaphors here, I know, but I like them both so will keep them) is very critical.

'It looks as if they don't intend to stay,' she says. 'They aren't bothering to make it into a home at all.'

Sarah, I will just tell you, is the daughter of another local farmer and she is, for all the energy she puts into matching towels in tapering piles in the bathroom, scented candles in the dining room, pelmets and tie-backs on the curtains in the living room, committed to the business of farming. She worked as hard on promoting a marriage between her brother and Mary, in the interests of economies of scale from the union of the two farms, as she did in turning the house into a show home. It was certainly not in the interests of either Mary or Sarah's brother, who had never a thought in common and who each chose for themselves partners as unlike each other as it is possible to be.

I don't share Sarah's view; Mary and Vassily are plain

ANNE YOUNGSON

people, plain speaking, indifferent to material comfort. The house suits them. They suit each other.

Vassily was there when I went to talk to Mary. We sat at their kitchen table drinking tea. I told them that a friend had asked my opinion about whether his daughter, who was unexpectedly pregnant by a man with whom she spent a passionate few days with no intention, on either side, of a longer relationship, should tell the comparative stranger he is about to become a father. They have a way of listening when I share news with them, or comment on something I have seen or heard, which is perfectly polite but which I feel implies they are waiting for me to finish speaking so they can go back to doing or thinking about whatever they were doing or thinking about before I spoke to them. This was not their reaction to Karin's story. They looked at me, as I was speaking, as though I was saying something of sufficient interest for them to concentrate, investigate, respond. They were not satisfied with the few details I had given them and I had to tell them the whole tale, as you told it to me.

Once they had all the information they needed, they were definite and articulate in their opinions. This was wonderful for me to listen to; you may remember I was concerned that the secret of their intimacy was that they did not bother to talk to each other very much, so did not fall out. Now I saw that their togetherness is so much more than this. It is based on a willingness to disagree with each other, and to enjoy doing it.

Mary is entirely on your daughter's side. Vassily believes as strongly that your daughter is wrong. Mary expressed the views you describe Karin as expressing. The mother has an absolute right, so Mary says, to decide for herself whether she

78

will have the child and also whether she will bring it up, or entrust its bringing up to someone else, or share the responsibility for bringing it up with someone else. Mary would not respect, she says, any woman who took these decisions without considering the impact on the child and anyone else who might have an interest in the child. She would have to know she could support it, care for it, avoid emotional damage to herself and others. She would have to know someone else had not had their life blighted because of the decision she had made. In this case, Mary says, Karin sounds like a woman perfectly capable of giving the child everything it might need – she sounds, she says, like a woman she would like to know – and the father cannot miss the child as he does not know of it and did not long for it. Mary would defend to the hilt the decision Karin has made.

But, said Vassily, she does not know enough to have the right to make this decision. She does not know if, for example, Ben has a mother living in Australia who is being denied, through Karin's selfishness, the right to know her own grandchild. She might, he said, becoming heated, have been denied grandchildren, to her great sorrow – and now she is old, ill perhaps, and this one piece of news, the chance she could have had to hold a baby in her arms, would have made her last months or years happy. (I had never suspected Vassily of such a vivid imagination but Mary told me later he had been thinking of his own grandmother, who was at the centre of the household he grew up in.) How would I feel, he wanted to know, if I had not been given the chance to know Tam and Sarah's children, to hold them as babies and enjoy them as individuals? Mary did not leave me space to say what I thought, which is that I am privileged to have this opportunity, but it is not a right; I am not defined as a grandmother and would not be diminished if I had no grandchildren.

'You are trumping her rights as a woman with the possible rights of another woman,' said Mary.

Vassily got up and walked about as if worried that his lack of ease in the English language would not adequately allow him to express the energy he wanted to put into his arguments. Karin, he said, was being disingenuous and manipulative in her attitude towards men in general and Ben in particular. She might assert her right to take her own decisions to ignore the rights which society would recognise the father as having, but she needed and used men for her own purposes and could not deny them recognition for the part they played. She had, he pointed out, been quick to use the protection Ben offered in the threatening situation she found herself in. Protection entirely based on his masculinity. Had she met a female friend, she might have felt slightly less vulnerable but she would not have felt safe, able to stride out with her head up, as she did when Ben was beside her.

And besides – he sat down again and took Mary's hand – what about the child? Did he or she not have a right to know his or her father?

'He or she will have that right,' said Mary. 'When he or she is old enough to understand. Rather that, than a childhood blighted by belonging in two places at once, travelling from parent and grandparent to another parent and grandparents, never quite understanding why she has to do this, whether it makes her less loved than her school friends, always believing the parent left behind is secretly pleased to see the back of her.'

They were enjoying this discussion with each other so

much I thought they had forgotten I was there, but then Vassily turned to me and said:

'You decide. The grandmother with no grandchildren, the child with no father, or the mother's right to manage her own life.'

By this time I had come to a conclusion and I will tell you, as I told them, what it is. We should look inside ourselves for fulfilment. It is not fair to burden children or grandchildren with the obligation to make us whole. Our obligation to them is to make them safe and provide them with an education. Karin can do that alone, if she chooses. She owes no one anything else. She owes it to herself to do what is best for her. When I had said this, Mary kissed me. I can't remember the last time she did that. Or the last time I enjoyed a conversation more.

I have some more thoughts on your last letter, but I will save them up so I can send you this quickly.

With love,
Tina

Silkeborg
1st August

Dear Tina,

I knew it was right to look forward to what you would have to say in answer to my last letter. Since I wrote to you, and you wrote back to me, I have been to spend a weekend in Copenhagen with Karin. I read your letter aloud to her. At first, she was cross with me because I had shared her story with strangers. But, I said to her, we can only choose how to act. We cannot choose how other people will judge the actions we take, what they will think, who they will speak to about them, what they will say. If she was not ashamed of her decision to have the baby and raise it alone, she should have no concern about who was told of this, how it was spoken of, these things she has no way of knowing or controlling. She agreed.

'Of course, I am never going to meet this woman or her daughter,' she said. It made me sad to think this might be so.

Then we discussed the arguments in your letter; your thoughts and what Mary and Vassily said. This was most helpful. We spoke at length about the other grandparents, about the child's need to know its father, about Karin herself and the ways in which she, for all her strength, might be vulnerable. Later, when she had had time to think over everything that had been said, Karin told me she had become concerned about what the child would want, when he reached an age to understand the absence of a father, and perhaps to ask questions. For this reason, she said, she had made the decision to stay in touch with Ben, to be sure she was in a position to find him, if it was important to her child's happiness that she could find him. She had been reluctant to reply to the e-mail he sent her, for fear of implying she might be looking for a longer-term relationship. Now, she thought this was selfish. She would reply. Carefully. With that, I am happy. And she is happy. I have never seen her with such a glow, but I am afraid I have not looked at her as closely as I should have done before.

We had a splendid weekend. She took me to Christiania and I took her to the Copenhagen Botanical Garden. When she suggested her outing, I did not want to go, but then I thought of the rows of raspberries and the need to pick as many as possible because there will be no second chance to go down the row, and I agreed. It was full of noise and colour. Everywhere, the walls were covered with pictures of dragons, faces with mouths wide open, goblins, mountains, all painted in bright, strong colours. In an ordinary street, I might have liked these pictures; they might have seemed bright and cheerful, but here they did not. Perhaps because there were too many of them, or because the buildings were so dirty and broken. This was once a military base, so it has no beauty of architecture – all the buildings are functional and the people who live here now do not care to make it smarter, or even to keep it as smart as it once was. It was earlier in the evening than when she had met Ben, not dark. Even so, I could see how menacing it would have been. I thought it was depressing, in spite of the colours. And there was too much noise. I lead a quiet life apart from when I choose to indulge myself with music, which is not the music I heard in Christiania. Except for one clarinettist playing Mozart, sitting on a folding chair. I paused to drop a coin into his open music case. A few streets further on, we came across a girl in a costume so strange I cannot describe it, with tattoos on her face, singing a song it was painful for me to listen to. Karin dropped a coin into the hat she had in front of her. I asked Karin if she preferred the song the girl sang to the tune the clarinettist played. No, she said.

'I preferred the Mozart, but I thought the girl performed the song better than the clarinettist performed the Mozart. She was interpreting the music she had chosen to perform with more skill and imagination.'

He was not a good clarinettist, I realised that. I had

rewarded him for playing a piece of music I like, but I could not have told you whether the girl was good at what she was doing, or not.

'Could I learn to appreciate the sort of song the girl sang?' I asked Karin.

'You don't need to,' she said. 'You have enough pleasure from the music you do understand; you don't need more.'

Perhaps this is right. There are only so many raspberries a man can eat.

We ate some food from a stall, sitting on a bench. I did not much like the food and have no way of describing it. A man – or possibly a woman – dressed as a clown, on stilts, walked past and leant down and plucked the last of whatever it was I was eating from my hand and carried it off. Karin laughed very much, and this made me happy.

When I suggested going to the Botanical Garden, I could see Karin hesitating as I had hesitated over Christiania, before she agreed. I was thinking of the unfurling fronds of ferns, but of course it is the wrong time of year for that. I had not understood how much else there would be to see and smell. The place was a surprise for us both. We had no idea what we were looking at, which, as you know, makes me uneasy. I like to be able to name things and I knew the names of nothing in the garden. Like the best museums, though, there were labels, full of information. Almost too much information. Each label told me what family the plant belonged to, and I started to compare one plant of the *rosaceae* family with another, quite dissimilar plant, and to speculate on what aspects of their taxonomy led to them being classified in the same family. Karin told me to stop doing this, because the plants were beautiful and what did it matter? But then she, too, became impatient when something she liked appeared to have no name. You see, I told her, names do matter.

'Names, yes,' she said. 'Otherwise I would have to say "the small tree with the soft green leaves and the lovely scented dark red and white flowers".'

We came across someone working in the garden who told us this was a *Clerodendrum trichotomum var fargesii*. He wrote it down for me. What is the family? I asked, and he told me there was some disagreement about that. Do you have such a tree?

We went into the glasshouse. It was warm and humid and the foliage and flowers of the plants in the glasshouse were lush (is that the word?). There was a spiral staircase leading to a gallery in the roof, and the feet of people going along this gallery looked like the shadows of birds flitting round the tops of the palms, but they were not. They were only feet. For all the efforts of the plants and the people who care for them to create the impression of a natural jungle, this was obviously indoors. I came to the garden in pursuit of the outdoors. We were too tired, by this time, to see all the outdoors. I will go back. When the fern fronds are unfurling, if not before.

Write soon.

Anders

Bury St Edmunds
10th August

Dear Anders,

I do have a *Clerodendrum trichotomum*, and I love it. It does not like our harsh winds, so I have it planted in a sheltered corner and it has grown to a lovely specimen. It is, as you say, a glorious thing, with a wonderful scent. It is very late to break, in the spring. The leaves are among the last in the garden to appear, and then they emerge slowly, so each year I fear my plant has been killed by the frost. But it is just reluctant to put on a show too early, I think. It is saving its strength to deliver up this great rush of flowers, holding them up above the leaves as if it is offering you bouquet after bouquet. I know nothing about plant families, but I am not surprised this plant is hard to pin down to one family or another. It is an individual.

Now, I just want to say a word or two about music. We are different in this; music obviously matters to you, but it is one of the raspberries I have missed on my way down the row. There is no music in my house and, day to day, I don't feel the lack of it, having never learnt to value it. But I have been conscious of having let it pass me by on the few occasions when it has been impossible for me not to notice it. (I hope you can pick your way through that double negative.) I can describe these times – two of them. There have been others but none so memorable.

I went to La Scala in Milan with Bella when she was living in Italy and I was visiting. We had neither of us seen an opera before, or listened to one, but she was trying to let me experience Italy and, at the same time, trying to keep herself from plunging headlong into despair over the situation she was in – manipulative ex-husband, tantalisingly close but only rarely seen daughter, living with a strange language, food, customs, smells – and buying tickets for the opera seemed like a good idea. It was a good idea, as far as I was concerned. We had seats near the top of the theatre where they were cheaper, but we wore our best frocks. Mine was a sleeveless dress – it was a hot evening – I had made myself from a black-and-white fabric bought in Norwich market. I was proud as can be of that dress: the way I looked in it; the careful construction of it; how it made me feel. I mention all this because it was part of the excitement of the occasion. We had our bottoms pinched several times before we reached our seats, and the people around us when we reached them were boisterous, noisy and exuberant, and altogether unlike the audience of any theatre I had been in before. The orchestra tuned up and the conductor was applauded onto the podium and before the overture even began I was as excited by the evening as if the main event was already happening. The first chords of the overture were almost an unwelcome interruption of my enjoyment of all these other sensations.

We were a long way from the stage and we had not bought the programme (which I would not have been able to read in any case), nor did we have the coins necessary to release the little opera glasses from the back of the seat in front. So I had no idea what was going on, which possibly made the spectacle and the music even more overwhelming than they would have been if I had been trying to follow the story. As it was, it mattered not at all that the story was unknown to me, or that I could not see the performers' faces. The sound was like a jet of cold, clean water scouring out an old feed bin; it was all that existed in the space it occupied. You will have better ways of describing the sensation of listening to such music, I'm sure. You have left yourself open to it, where I have not.

The opera was *Madama Butterfly*, which was an unlucky choice, not musically but as regards the story. We were all right for the first act, which neither of us understood, and we drank the wine we had brought with us in an old water bottle in the first interval and it seemed we were having a good time. I mean, I was definitely having a good time, and Bella managed to behave as if the same was also true for her. In the second act, opaque as the plot was, we realised that Butterfly was an abandoned wife and, worse, she had a child. By the second interval, Bella was in a state, and the rest of the lukewarm wine only made it worse. She was being assaulted by the music, she said. It was teasing her with its beauty and mocking her with its sadness. When the lights went down again, the final act – you probably know the opera – begins with a wordless, hummed chorus while Butterfly waits for news of her faithless husband. I could feel Bella starting to shake, beside me. Her head fell forward and when I took her hand, it was wet with the tears she had been wiping away. Cold tears, raising goose bumps on my warm, bare arms. I had no option but to help her past the half-dozen very irritated Italians to the end of the row and down the stairs to the street. We sat on the steps of the opera house, Bella sobbing and me outwardly calm but inwardly yearning after the music I had been snatched away from. We were still sitting there when the performance ended and the doors opened and bursts of excited Italian drove us to our feet.

I promised myself, as we walked back to Bella's flat, that I would go, as soon as I could, to another production of *Madama Butterfly*. I never have. I have never been to another live opera. I bought a CD but the first time I put it on, Edward was in the room. He could see no possible reason why I should want to listen to 'that noise', and I could not even pretend, in the face of his disapproval, in my own living room, that I was enjoying it. I played it sometimes in the car, on my own, but I began to think I had been utterly misled by the occasion, by the dress, the Italians, the heat, by Bella, and in truth I would hate an opera if I went to one in dull, cold England as much as Edward thought I should do. So I have never tried. I have never been back to see if this was a raspberry worth searching for among the leaves.

My experience of live pop music is just as limited. Bella and I went to some pubs with live bands playing a few times, and were as fervent as any other teenagers in our devotion to the groups or singers we saw on television, but I had not been to anything approaching a pop concert for decades, until a couple of years ago. My second son, Andrew, has a sideline in providing straw bales to events. We have always sold a few of the small, oblong bales, ones the size a man (or a woman, me for instance) can lift, to local fairs for seating, and to back-yard chicken farmers. Andrew, though, has built up quite a business hiring out bales for big occasions – weddings, pop festivals and so on. He builds structures, at a cost: straw castles, forts, cottages. He is the mechanical one in the family. He looks after all the machinery. When Tam is reading about crop rotation, Andrew is looking at the specification of the latest in harvesting equipment. He is more of a mystery to me than the other two, and heaven knows they are mysterious enough. I assume Andrew is happy: he never appears to be unhappy and his enthusiasm for complex pieces of engineering is real enough, but is it enough to sustain him, I wonder. He is very private. He lives in the farmhouse still but has constructed a separate entrance for his room, which is over the kitchen and approached by its own staircase. He has turned a window into a doorway and erected a wooden ladder up to it, so it can be reached without even entering the house. So I know almost nothing of what he does with himself when he is not in a tractor cab or the machinery shed. Except that he goes off with a low loader and a trailer full of bales, from time to time, with a couple of mates and any other equipment he needs to move them into position.

On this occasion, it was a pop festival not too far away, but far enough that they wanted to camp out there, so they needed someone to follow them in a car with all their camping gear and food and so on. I think I went because I was the only person available who was insured to drive the only car available. Although Andrew might have chosen me as the person he wanted to come along. I can't be sure. I was quite intimidated at the idea of the enormous site and all the young people, as I drove towards it. I had an image of what it would be like, from television reporting of festivals, and I could imagine the confidence and bounce of the festival-goers, their air of knowing all they needed to know to control their own destinies. Older people go to festivals too, older than I am, but none of them, I felt sure, would be wearing a fleece with the name of an agricultural feed merchant on it. I would have felt happier in a hand-made patchwork skirt and my hair in plaits, but I don't own one, or have long enough hair.

Of course, when we got there, it was before the event started and I felt foolish for having had all these thoughts on the way. The place was full of all manner of people working away to put up tents and stages, toilets and food stalls. If you had lined up everyone on the site that first day, I would have been the least remarkable. It is often the case, that when I am most anxious about how I will be remarked upon by other people, I turn out to be the most likely not to be noticed at all.

I stayed for the whole day, providing food and hot drinks to Andrew and his friends as they moved the bales into position and fashioned a castle, with battlements reached by a staircase of small bales with wooden boards on top, to form the steps. When they had finished, I climbed up to the top and looked down at the activity below me, then out at the flat, flat land, the green and gold of the crops in the field, the dark mass of trees and thick black lines of hedges. They had taken so much time to build the castle that the first acts were tuning up as we sat on the top. They wouldn't be opening the structure to visitors until the next morning, so we had the grandstand view all to ourselves. The atmosphere was changing as darkness fell, and the people working with purpose finished their tasks and the crowd of people looking only for pleasure grew larger and larger below us. Then the music started and I was too enthralled to leave. I stayed until Edward, not normally an anxious man, phoned to ask what exactly I thought I was doing, staying away so long. I knew what it was I was doing. I was being absorbed, mind, body and spirit, into the vibrations created by the music and the crowd; I was wired up to the energy of thousands of people sharing the sound. If I looked beyond the edge of the festival site, before the light faded, at the surrounding farmland, and tried to imagine that music being created with only the fields around it, without the pack of people in constant motion, the smells of the food cooking, the occasional shouts and cries and laughter from festival-goers arriving late, it would have been no more than noise. And it was so much more than noise. It was utterly absorbing, but even as I was part of it, before I climbed down the straw staircase and into the car to drive back to the farm, I felt as if this was something I had missed. Unlike the opera, which I held out for myself the promise of finding again, I thought this was something it was too late for me to be part of the way the people on the ground below me were part of it – whether they were young or old, they were, I felt sure, able to understand and experience what was happening here in a way I could not. But I did feel this once.

It is important not to be too greedy, as you say. Enjoy the raspberries you have found. I can see the *Clerodendrum* in flower from the window as I write this.

Write soon,
Love,
Tina

Silkeborg
17th August

Dear Tina,
You understand music even though you have had so little to do with it. You describe so well the sensations of being involved with the sound of live music, when it is in a big space, or there are many, many instruments or voices creating it. As I told you, I sing in a choir and we perform in the largest church in Silkeborg. It is not because the music we are singing glorifies God; it is just the best place in Silkeborg for choirs to sing. When I am performing I feel, as you describe it, 'wired up' to the energy of the people singing around me. (I am hoping my English is improving as I write to you. If it is, it will be because you use such expressive language and I am catching the rhythm of it, as I catch the rhythm of the music from the other members of the choir. Perhaps we are beginning to sing in tune?)

In July the choir put on a concert of light opera. Songs by Hoffmann, Lehár, Danish folk songs. They were cheerful, tuneful songs and easy to sing, easy to listen to. It is the kind of music I might sing to myself, though not out loud, as a distraction from the wind or the rain as I pedal to work. That is, not grand or uplifting, but comforting. The church was full every night with people who had paid for a seat, and this is not always so. Also, the audience was happy, applauding loudly and asking for encores. This, too, does not always happen. The concert finished before dark, which comes late in July, and while it was still warm enough to walk around the streets and sit outside the cafes. The audience and the performers came out into the square in front of the church and mixed in with the other residents of Silkeborg already there, enjoying the warmth and the light, sitting in the cafes and bars and talking about the music they had heard. Altogether, you could say, as the director of the choir did say, to us and to the newspapers, it was a big success and brought happiness and laughter not only into the church but also to Silkeborg town centre. But, although it was enjoyable, I do not think it was the same as the sensation you describe when you visited the opera and went to the festival. It was too simple.

I prefer the concerts that have more complex music, maybe less tuneful, harder to learn, harder to sing, harder, I suppose, to listen to. Then I am buried in the notes and the other voices producing a harmony that seems to occur without any of us making an effort to produce it. I am outside myself and inside the music. I have never expressed this before.

As a rule, we, the choir members, meet together and rehearse, meet together and perform. Some of the members are friends or become friends. Most of us talk to each other only about the music or the small problems of being part of the choir – the cold draughts in winter, the lack of time and so on. I wonder if Jürgen, who stands to the left of me, and is an engineer with an electricity company, or Martin, who stands to the right of me, a teacher of history, feel as I do. I should ask them. But I am not likely to do that. It is partly because they would think it unlikely I would do that which makes it unlikely I will. We may want to be other than we are, but we do not want to unsettle the opinion people have already formed; maybe to replace it with a lesser opinion.

I understand why it was not possible for you to enjoy the CD of *Madama Butterfly*, hearing it in fragments, with distractions, when the music is new to you. You need to discover it, first. To listen to it with proper attention. Then, when it has become familiar, each note will unfold as you expect it to and you can take pleasure from hearing just a few bars, because you will have a memory of the beauty of the whole piece.

I have a photo of my unborn grandchild. His (or maybe her – Karin knows the answer but has not told me) face and skull have something of the Tollund Man about them. Essential. Reduced to the elements of what is human, but so powerfully present it is amazing to feel I cannot at once reach out a hand and hold his.

Write soon.

Anders

Bury St Edmunds
23rd August

Dear Anders,

There is a rumpus in our house. It turns out that Sarah was right – though I still think her deduction was faulty. Mary and Vassily do not intend to stay. They have bought a plot of land on the outskirts of Inverness and they are planning to live in a caravan while Vassily builds them a house on it. Mary has accepted a job with a firm of accountants in Inverness and will come out of the caravan each morning in high heels and a white blouse, with a briefcase, and will go into the town. Vassily will come out in his overalls and set the cement mixer going.

They arranged all this during a couple of trips to Scotland that the rest of us assumed were just holidays taken up with walking and sightseeing and drinking whisky. Edward is beside himself. (What an odd phrase that is, but I can't think of another way to put it. It implies a mixture of anger and frustration that gnaws away at you until you cannot comfortably occupy the space your body takes up.) For one thing, he believes they have behaved in an underhand way by arranging it without telling anyone – that is to say, without telling him – what they had in mind. It would have surprised me if they had told us. They are not given to chatting about themselves (or anything else) and if they had overcome their natural reserve, then letting Edward know in advance would have unleashed an unbearable torrent of words. Many of them abusive. My husband has never understood the distinction between talking to people and talking at them.

Edward's second complaint about Mary and Vassily is that they are leaving him in the lurch. This is a more serious aspect, as far as he is concerned. They do not leave for another month but however much time he had, it would never be enough to find a replacement accountant to do the books, or a replacement handyman to do the chores.

The third, and most serious, issue is that it will cost him

money. Mary and Vassily were comparatively cheap. It does mean, I point out to him, that we can generate an income by letting the cottage they have been living in. This does not mollify him. He despises the money gained by, as he puts it, 'farming tourists'. It is an effete sort of way of making a living, suitable for people raised in towns who don't like hard work. Not to be compared with money made by sitting in a tractor cab and claiming subsidies. Not as satisfying as saving expense by extracting labour from your family at little or no cost. I know that letting out holiday homes is hard work, because I do most of it. It is fruitless to say so. Because the real objection Edward has to this particular piece of diversification is that he doesn't like the guests. Whoever they are. He does not want them in his farmyard, however pleasant, interesting and interested they might be. And many of them are all three. He prefers the ones who stay indoors all day watching television. There is enjoyment to be had from despising them.

For the first time I am thinking I may not send you the letter I am writing. I am ashamed of myself for expressing so much bitterness. Only, I do hate conflict. (I can picture my mother nodding, knowingly.) I am weary of trying to smooth things over.

If I destroyed the first half of this letter, it would be to disguise myself from you, and I do not want to do that, so I will send it. I wrote it all down after the news had been broken and the storm was raging. I will carry on now, in a calmer way.

When I think back to what I have said to you about my children and the way I have thought about them, which I only properly understood by writing to you, I realise that I have been wrong to believe they were happy to have grown up on the farm and to be living and working as adults on the farm. I have spoken to Mary and asked her: Why? Why go? Why Inverness? She said:

'Because I want to know what it is like to live somewhere else. To live in a city. To work in an office.'

'And if you don't like it?' I said.

'Then we can change,' she said, smiling at me. 'Whatever. Nothing is so fixed it cannot be altered.'

Did I know that, when I was her age? Do I believe it, even now? As she said these words, the picture in my mind was of the Tollund Man, still and silent, fixed firmly for millennia in his bed of peat. Then I thought of the words we have used to each other, you and I, in describing our lives – mine bound up in the relentless timetable of food production, yours buried in the fossilised remains of the past. It is hard for us to say, isn't it, that nothing is so fixed it cannot be altered? The seasons do not linger, waiting for it to be convenient for the sowing and the harvesting. The artefacts you study are what they are. They represent a moment in time. They have no scope for change; that is why you study them. That is why they are useful for telling us things we might otherwise never have known. I begin to think we have been misled by the types of lives we lead into overlooking our personal potential to be other than we have always been.

I have thoughts to share with you about music and about the likeness of a baby in the womb, but I will save these up. I will be joyful in my next letter. I will find something to point out to you. 'Look at that!' I will say, and I will be happy to imagine you looking at it. I can't tell if you are beginning to write like me; I don't know how I write. The words just tumble out onto the page. When I read the words you write back, they sound like you, singing in a tune I have become familiar with and which is therefore comforting.

Love,
Tina

Silkeborg
30th August

Dear Tina,

I love the words you use. I have had to buy a bigger English dictionary to be sure I have understood everything you say to me. Rumpus. This is not a word I have heard before and I am pleased to have met it. I have looked it up in my dictionary and it tells me it means a noisy or violent disturbance. It is enjoyable both as a sound and as a word meaning something I did not previously have a precise name for. There was a rumpus in the museum yesterday, which I will tell you about. But first, your daughter's decision to go to Scotland.

Like your husband's three reasons for not liking her decision, I have three reasons you might consider this change to be a good thing. Number one, you will have somewhere to visit. I have the pleasure of the journey and experiencing the difference between the places my children live and the place I live, as well as the joy of their company when I reach them.

Secondly, there are mountains in Scotland, and do you not sometimes long for mountains? We both live where there are none and, although I would not want to live among them, I love the way they make me feel when I visit them. When I was twenty years old, I had a friend who took up mountain climbing. He was attracted to all dangerous sports – bob-sleigh, hang-gliding – and for the sake of our friendship, I did several things I would never otherwise have done, and do not wish to do again. When he started climbing, I went with him to the Alps. I have never forgotten the feeling of being on the extreme edge of the world, only the rock face so close and the valley so far, far away, and in between, nothing at all, only air and sky. I recover something of the thrill of those moments when I come among mountains. I remember the fear as well, of course, and am pleased I do not have to experience that again.

In the third place, you told me how happy it made you to see your daughter happy in her new marriage, and how this was something you had wanted for her and had not known how to give her. With this move to Scotland, is she not stepping deeper and deeper into happiness and fulfilment? After finding someone as a lover and companion, going with him to explore other ways of life than the one she has always known? I think so.

Now, the rumpus. I was walking through the museum, going back to my office after a meeting to discuss money. Much of the work I do is involved with money. It is not my job to raise money or to manage it, but day to day it is the matter always under consideration. Sometimes there are meetings about what the museum might buy, or special exhibitions, and I enjoy these, even if the discussion is mostly about the cost. The cost is important and cannot be ignored. But most meetings are about how to make a budget stretch around all the things that need to be done – cleaning, maintenance – and still leave something over to progress the real work of the museum. This meeting, yesterday, was one of those.

It was in our new building, where the Tollund Man is kept, and my office is upstairs in the old part (very old, in comparison to the rest of Silkeborg, but still built seventeen hundred years after the Tollund Man died). There is an open green space between the two, with benches where visitors can sit and enjoy the sun, and I was looking forward to the brightness, after the gloom of the meeting room. Also I wanted to hurry back to be doing the work I like to do, so I was walking quickly towards the door when I heard the most desolate wailing from the room where the Tollund Man is on display. It was a child crying. I had been thinking, for much of the meeting, of the image of Karin's baby. I have it in my briefcase now. (With the feather from a wing of a female pheasant. Both things make me happy.) I had been thinking about the image as a child I will one day know, but also of the likeness of this image of someone not yet born to the body of the Tollund Man, centuries dead. Because I had been thinking in this way, the sound of a child crying from the room where the Tollund Man lies made me turn aside to find out what it was that made this child so unhappy.

A little girl in a very pretty dress was standing in front of the Tollund Man weeping as if she had no hope of ever being comforted. Her mother was talking to her, holding her hand, trying to soothe her. A museum attendant was close by with his arms folded, asking the mother to please prevent her child from upsetting the other visitors. By the time I arrived, the girl was almost exhausted and had, in any event, started to sob and hiccup in place of wailing. I asked the mother what it was that had caused her such grief and she said:

'She wants the Tollund Man to wake up and talk to her.

The lady at the desk said she would be able to ask him questions, and she doesn't understand why he can't answer. She thought maybe he was just asleep and I told her he was never going to wake up.'

I should explain that there is an interactive panel outside the room where he is kept, and it is possible to find out more information from this, about the Iron Age, about the body, about the process of finding and preserving him and so on, by tapping on the question marks. This is what the receptionist would have meant when she told the girl she could ask a question.

'He could be asleep,' I said. 'I have often wished he would wake up and talk to me. He looks like someone I would have liked to know.' The little girl had stopped making a noise and was looking up at me, but with tears still falling down her face. 'What did you want to ask him?' I said.

She put her face against the sleeve of her mother's cardigan. Her mother took a tissue from her pocket and cleaned the little girl's face. The child looked up at me again when this was done and said:

'I wanted him to tell me a story.'

'That's what I want, too,' I said. 'We can never know what stories he might have told us if he was able to wake up.'

'Do you think he will, one day?' asked the little girl.

'No,' I said. 'I don't think he wants to wake up. His life will have been quite hard. Not like yours. Cruel things will have happened to him. He is peaceful now, look. We should let him be.'

'We could tell him a story,' said her mother. 'He might like to listen to one of our stories, even if he can't tell us one of his.'

She sat down on the floor, cross-legged with the child in her lap, and began to recite a story. It is not one I had heard or read before, but it was a good story so I will repeat it to you, as nearly as I can in the way the mother told it.

There was once a man made entirely of rags. His head was a ball of dishcloths; his hair was strips of flannel, some of them black, some of them yellow. His clothes were like a waterfall of pieces of fabric in every colour, every pattern, every size, every shape. His hands and feet were pieces of stiff canvas; his eyes were scraps of bright blue silk; his mouth was a crescent of scarlet velvet, upturned in a permanent smile. When the Rag Man first arrived in the town, the children who had not been properly brought up threw things at him, and the parents who thought nothing mattered as much as being clean and tidy locked their front gates so the Rag Man could not come in and sleep under the bushes in their gardens. Even the children who were properly brought up and the parents who thought nothing mattered as much as hugs and laughter did not quite like to go close to the Rag Man. He went to live in the park, where there was a big, round lake and plenty of trees, and no one much bothered with him.

Then one day people started talking about the Rag Man again. 'Have you seen,' they said to each other, 'what's happening to him?' Each time they saw him, he had fewer rags. His locks of flannel hair had reduced to just a few strands. His clothes were nothing but bits and pieces of dull, white sheeting; even his face looked thinner, as if a layer or two of dishcloth had been peeled away.

'He's even more scruffy and disgusting than he was,' said

the badly-brought-up children and the obsessively clean parents.

'He looks sad,' said the well-brought-up children and the loving parents.

When the people of the town were all gathered on the streets waiting for the celebrations for the National Day in that country to start, they talked about the Rag Man, and a woman whose husband had recently died said:

'I feel so guilty, now. I should never have accepted the piece of cloth he gave me to dry my tears, but it reminded me of a shirt I once made for my husband and it made me think of happier days. It gave me such comfort.'

'I feel the same,' said a man standing near her, whose house had burnt down, leaving him with nowhere to live but an old shed in his garden. 'I was in despair and the Rag Man gave me a square of dishcloth to wipe my face, and when I looked at it, I knew I should pull myself together. At least, I thought, I could keep my shed clean and that would give me back some self-respect. I felt better at once.'

So it went on – up and down the street people confessing they had taken the rags the Rag Man offered them. It seemed that anyone in the town who was grieving or cast down would go to the park to walk round the lake and be alone with their misery and their regrets. After a while, the Rag Man would come out of the trees and pluck a piece of rag from his clothes, his hair or his face and offer it to them as you might offer a handkerchief to someone you see crying. In each case, the rag made them think positive thoughts and from that moment, although they were still sad, they felt able to go back out of the park and carry on with life.

Soon everyone in the crowd was telling a story, or listening to a story, about the kindness of the Rag Man, and when the brass band had played and the children had danced and the miraculous pumpkin – which was the symbol of this proud country (because of the legend of brave men hiding in a giant pumpkin and leaping out to save the nation from invaders) – had been paraded past the crowds, the mayor stood up and made an announcement.

'The Rag Man is giving himself away, rag by rag, to help others,' he said. 'It is up to us to give him back what he has lost.'

The people came from all over the town, even the ones who used to scorn the Rag Man – for they have tragedies too, and want comfort – and left the cloth they no longer needed or could spare on the path beside the lake. After this, the Rag Man became as colourful, as plump and as ragged as he had been before. Now the townspeople could recognise, in his costume, pieces of fabric they knew. Scraps of the old curtains from the theatre, the remains of canvas kneelers from the church, the awning that used to hang over the butcher's window. Now everyone loves the Rag Man, especially those who have been unhappy, and isn't everyone unhappy, sometimes?

Everybody in the room was still, smiling at the child and her mother telling the remains of an Iron Age man with his perfectly preserved face a story he could never have imagined. When it was finished, the little girl said:

'Can we have an ice cream now?' and walked away with her mother.

I looked at the Tollund Man's face and imagined the leathery skin was old cleaning cloth and his smile was stitched on. I wish we knew the circumstances of his death. Not the details of how he died, which we do know, but the hours and days before it happened. Did he come forward as a sacrifice for the good of others, as the Rag Man did, or was his death a punishment for a crime the people he lived among could not forgive? I think you were crying, in a way, when you first wrote, because you felt the Tollund Man should be able to wake up and tell you stories that would help. Instead, we are telling each other stories. I am happy that it is so.

Write soon. Think mountains.

Love,

Anders

Bury St Edmunds
6th September

Dear Anders,

All is calm. You will see that this is a letter, in an envelope, and this is because I have something to send you. I will explain.

Thank you for the story. When I had read it I went to the chest where I keep all the old pieces of fabric and clothes I know I will never use or wear again but which I cannot bear to throw out. My brother's bedroom curtains are in there. They have a grey background and a pattern of black sailing boats with blue or red sails, made simple in the way an Impressionist painter might make them simple, not like a cartoonist would. My sister and I had pink curtains with flowers on and as a child I was frustrated that I was not allowed to have curtains like my brother's, which you could look at again and again and each time the boats would be different. Sometimes they looked ready to sail away and sometimes they looked fixed and sullen. Sometimes they did not look like boats at all but like lines and shapes that could be anything you wanted them to be. When my mother redecorated the room I asked for the curtains and meant to hang them in this attic bedroom where I have my sewing machine and my desk, where I write these letters, but they did not fit the windows and I prefer not to have curtains up here, but to be able to see the sky, without impediment. So I put them away in the chest.

The dress I told you about, the one that I wore to the opera with Bella, is also in the chest. There is a scarf Bella bought once, when we were together, that is cerise silk with a pattern of small sequins sewn on to it. She decided almost at once that it did not suit her, and tied it round my neck instead. I wore it all that day, but never again. I love it for how vibrant it is, how exuberant, and I can imagine it might suit me, if I had the other clothes to wear with it that would make it look like a carnation in a bowl of mixed garden flowers. If I wore it with the clothes I own, it would look like a carnation in a bowl of dried leaves.

Perhaps I should stop thinking 'dress', 'scarf', 'curtain' when I look at these things, and think 'rag', then turn them into patchwork. Having thought this, I have snipped off a bit of the curtains to send you, as I cannot paint a good enough picture with words.

What I wanted to say about music is not about music at all, but about poetry. It is a part of my life as music is a part of yours. This is something else I feel I owe to the Tollund Man. I might never have started to read poetry if Seamus

Heaney had not written a poem about him. Bella found it in a library book and copied it out for me. This handwritten sheet is on my wall today, the description of his 'peat-brown head' alongside the picture of it. Since then, poetry has become my music. I read randomly, but the poets I love tell me something about how they experience, for example, grief, or loneliness, or a moment of joy. My choice of what to read is random because I buy all my books of poetry from an Oxfam charity shop in town that sells only second-hand books. A woman whose name, I am ashamed to admit, I don't know, but who loves poetry, volunteers there on a Thursday. Whenever I am in town on a Thursday, I go in and she shows me all the poetry books that have been donated since last I visited, and recommends the ones she thinks I will like. She is usually right. I have a collection now, mainly modern, by poets not all of whom are well known. Some of them, for all I know, not even very good in the judgement of those who are more literate than I am. So what I wanted to say was that I understand what you mean about having to know a piece to be able to snatch pleasure from it in passing, as it were. Then it can hum away in the background, ready to be pulled up to the surface for half a minute or half an hour or however long is available or necessary. A poem will seize a thought or an idea that can keep me occupied for ten times the time it took to read. I have something to think about while my arms and legs are employed doing the things I do every day. The poems I know well, and love best, I do not need to read. I can catch a couple of lines off a page or from memory, and the pleasure of the whole poem is there. When I read poems new to me, I have to read them slowly and carefully, and, if it is a poem I particularly like, several times. Then at last it may become one of those I know so well I only have to let the book fall open at the page as I walk past, between washing line and ironing board, and in the length of time it takes to switch the basket of washing from one hip to the other, I will have taken in the sense and beauty of a line or two and it will sustain me.

Do you read poetry?

When I had my children, we were not given prints of the scans showing them as foetuses in the womb. But my daughter-in-law had prints of my grandchildren from her scans, and I have them pinned on the board here in my attic workroom. Even now they have been born and have turned into people I know and love, I still keep those first pictures of them, though I cannot say I look at them or even notice them, much of the time. I lined them up on my desk, when I'd read your letter, and I can see exactly what you mean. It is not just the essential appearance of something human yet not quite of this world. The pictures also hold a promise of someone not quite knowable yet capable of being known.

Mary and Vassily are almost ready to leave. They have packed the few things they want to take and have organised a farewell party. I had expected them to slide off with no goodbyes. I could picture them opening the door of their cottage before dawn and putting their few belongings in the back of Vassily's van. I imagined waking just as it grew light, at the sound of the engine, and watching the van moving slowly away from me through the gate. In fact, I realise, I am forever interpreting their disdain for social chitchat as a reluctance to engage, a positive avoidance of others. In truth they do not avoid others. They have friends. They make choices about who to meet, who to talk to, on the basis of who they want to meet and talk to. What they avoid is idle conversation with people they have no interest in talking to. So there will be a party. I am cooking food for it. I have consulted with Vassily who has described the food his mother and grandmother cooked for celebrations in his home in Lithuania, and I have downloaded recipes from the internet. The food is heavy on root vegetables and will probably suit my family's tastes, which tend to favour bulk over subtlety, but just in case I will also cook pizza and sausage rolls. Otherwise I am worried there will be nothing they will want to eat and I am compelled to provide them with food they will eat. It is a self-propelled compulsion. I could say: 'This is what I have cooked and there is no other food, so you must eat it.' But I am not able to do this.

Meanwhile, the replacements for Vassily and Mary have been selected and are even now, as I look out of the window, being towed back and forth across the yard by Edward and Tam, being taught the business of the farm. This is not truly necessary in either case. Instead of Vassily we will have Gregor, who is also Lithuanian and a friend of Vassily's, a cousin even, I think. He has turned up whenever a job Vassily was doing needed two people; was best man at the wedding; is exactly like Vassily in being dark and quiet but smiles more and sings, quietly, as he works. Though I will miss Vassily, I am pleased to think I will be seeing Gregor more regularly, as he walks around with a toolbox and a ladder.

I cannot say the same of the woman who will do the job Mary used to do. Her name is Daphne Trigg; she is nearer to me than to Mary in age and utterly unlike both of us. She is the sensible choice, because she has been doing some basic bookkeeping for us since March, when Mary became busy with the preparations for her wedding, so she does not need guidance from the start. Mary did not want to choose Daphne, on the basis of competence. Daphne, Mary says, is not very good at bookkeeping; will make mistakes; will leave work for the accountant who audits the books to do, at additional expense. I did not want to choose her, either, as, unlike Mary, Vassily and Gregor, Daphne does not wait until she has something worth saying before she opens her mouth. She is also physically incongruous in the purposeful setting of a working farm, where everything is arranged around getting the job done and everywhere is only as clean as it needs to be, where everyone moves briskly, wearing clothes and shoes suitable for somewhere only as clean as it needs to be. Daphne is a fleshy woman, slightly pink. She doesn't always wear pink and her hair is dyed bronze, but she creates a pink impression on me. She does not appear to own a pair of wellington boots or even a pair of shoes with laces and with soles that grip in the mud. However, all this is of no relevance in this decision (and much of what I have just said is too prejudiced and petty to be allowed to count). We have gone ahead with appointing Daphne despite Mary's reservations, because she is available. Also, Edward says it is the right thing to do because Daphne's husband, a golfing partner of Edward's, died last year and poor Daphne needs the money and the occupation in her newly widowed state. I suspect the decision also feels right to him because, like Gregor, she is cheap (on the face of it).

*

I am comforted by the thought of mountains. Write soon.
    Love,
    Tina

Silkeborg
18th September

Dear Tina,

I read your description of the fabric without unfolding the tissue paper round the sample. It was as the words you used led me to expect it to be. I took it out of my briefcase at work and left it on my desk when I was called away. When I returned a colleague was waiting for me and she pointed at the piece of cloth and asked what I meant to do with it. What was it for? I said I was going to do nothing with it. It was not for anything. It was a piece of cloth and that was enough. She said she did not like the pattern, which did not surprise me. Her house, I expect, and my house would be so different from yours. If I understand correctly the things you have said. Let me describe my house.

It was built within the last forty years and is a simple design. The rooms are large and there are few of them. On the ground floor, just the kitchen and a living space and a dining space. Upstairs, bedrooms and bathrooms. All the walls are white. I have no curtains, only blinds. In the living space there is a large, soft sofa facing a stove, and also some firmer chairs shaped like eggs. This is a standard Danish design. The lights are dramatic. The main light is also a standard Danish design. Many of the houses I go into have the same one, like an inverted flower opening its petals. There are floor lamps that make me think of willow trees, bending over to let light fall in a pool around themselves. (I read back what I have just written and I have used nature to describe what is in fact completely unnatural.) The floor is wooden and there are rugs. In the dining space is a black wood table, black wood chairs. On a stretch of wall under the staircase I have my desk facing the wall, where I am writing this. There is a bookcase, a low table and another piece of furniture where things are kept out of sight. I don't know what you would call it. All this is pleasant and restful and could be any of my neighbours' houses as well as my own. On the surfaces, on the bookcase and the windowsills and other pieces of furniture, are one or two photographs, which is also usual, I think. Otherwise, there is what Birgitt chose to keep, out of the things she picked up, and bring into the house and display. Everything else I have described was chosen by me. At the time we first moved here we maintained a pretence that we were making decisions together, but in fact she agreed with all of my suggestions. My suggestions were based on what I saw in the houses of friends and in the rooms laid out as examples at the furniture store.

Here is what Birgitt added:

A piece of broken pottery with a cream background and what might be a peacock's tail, folded up, painted across it from top to bottom.

A collection of pebbles in different sizes, shapes and colours. Birgitt moved these every week, when she cleaned, rearranging them as a group or separating them into several groups. They have stayed in the arrangement they were in when we left for our anniversary trip. I know the pattern they make by heart, so I can move them, to clean, and put them back as they were.

A dented brass padlock, with its key in the lock. It is open.

A bowl made out of the hoof of some large animal. I don't know what. It is very ugly.

A piece of wood shaped by the sea to form a perforated, twisted arch. It is very beautiful.

A slice from the trunk of a tree that has been felled, very thin but wide, showing the circles of the tree's growth becoming smaller and smaller towards the centre.

A box made from playing cards. Every suit and every card is represented, but not every card in every suit. It is quite old and rather dirty.

A fan so torn only the skirt of a gown and the curls of a wig show it was once decorated with scenes from the eighteenth century.

A tower of buttons; a large scarlet one at the bottom and then smaller and less and less colourful ones until the top of the tower, which is a tiny, transparent button.

A collection of twigs caught together in a sort of birdcage shape. I am careful with this. It is fragile.

Birgitt never explained anything in the list I have just written out for you. Never spoke about the objects at all, and I did not mind because I accepted them as significant in themselves, for her sake. Now I think perhaps I would have been more use to her if I had insisted she talk to me about them. They never formed a link between us as this piece of material, with the history you have given me of why it matters to you, forms a link between you and me. I am beginning to think that these objects, which I have dusted and arranged so carefully since her death, have no meaning, and I should throw away the ones I do not like to look at. I will ask Karin and Erik. They are both coming to stay next weekend. This does not often happen and I am excited about it. I can see that cooking for your family is important to you, and I will cook for mine.

I will let you know if I am successful. With the cooking and with throwing things out. I do not read poetry; another raspberry not yet picked but still on the plant, and I will go back along the row to find it.

Love,
Anders

Bury St Edmunds
27th September

My dear Anders,
If I were to take one of the rooms in our house and make a list of all the furniture and the objects in it, I would need a spreadsheet. The task would only be manageable if I could put them into categories first – the useful and used; the useful but not used; ornaments, whole; ornaments, broken; items belonging elsewhere; random.

Having written this list of categories, I went through to a room we call the parlour. This is a pretentious word for it, but it has been known as that by previous generations and so it still is. This is the room where we sit, in the evening, where we entertain friends. It is warm in the winter and cool in the summer and I chose this room because it is the most formal and therefore the least cluttered. As soon as I was in it, with my list, I realised I could not begin to make order out of chaos with the categories I had invented. This must be making you smile, you who are a master of cataloguing, sorting, sifting, putting item a) with item b) into a family. I looked first at a green glass vase. I do not use it to put flowers in, partly because I rarely have flowers to put in it, though I could have if I bothered to grow and pick them for the purpose of brightening up the house, but also because it is cracked and the water seeps out. Is this 'useful but not used' or is it 'ornaments, broken'? I think perhaps I should begin with two headings: 'Broken' and 'Whole' and then have sub-categories underneath. I am happy that the vase would then slot neatly into 'Broken – useful but not used'. There again, it is only in the parlour because I like it. The green is a pretty green and the shape is elegant. So is it, after all 'Broken – ornament'?

How do you do your job? I'm looking at a bootlace. Unused. Just the one, left behind by someone who has brought a packet of two new laces into the parlour to replace a broken lace, and did not bother to remove the one he did not need. I imagine I will have picked up and thrown out the remains of the old one in my passes through the room with a duster and a vacuum cleaner, but the unused bootlace cannot be thrown out. It needs to be picked up and taken back to the drawer in the scullery where anything to do with shoes is kept. I could pick it up now, but then I would have to go through the hall, along a corridor, across the kitchen and down some steps to the scullery, and it seems a lot of time and effort for one bootlace. If I look around I can see other things that need to be picked up and carried to where they ought to be, and put away: a pair of gloves, a pair of scissors, a manual for a dehumidifier, the cover of a smoke alarm, a glasses case (empty), an elastic band, an elastic bandage, a biscuit barrel (empty), a penknife, two golf tees. None of these belongs in the scullery. If I were to carry them all at once (for which I would first need to fetch a basket or bag) I would have to travel through every room on the ground floor, up the stairs to the first floor and again to the second floor and finally out to the farm office in the yard, in order to put them all back where they belong. Why bother?

Even if I managed to rid the room of things left behind there would still be – I have been back down there to count – eight chairs, two sofas, three small tables, four other pieces of furniture for, as you put it, keeping things out of sight. Also on the floor, which is stone flags covered in rugs with frayed edges, are three other objects for keeping things in – logs, magazines, knitting. On the wall are eight pictures, all of them so murky it is hard to say what they are meant to represent; three of them appear to be paintings of livestock, two are of trees, three of people's faces. If I wanted to know more, I would need to take them outside into the sunlight, or bring in a torch to shine on them, as the windows in this room are small, and the only lighting – apart from the floor lamp I use to let me see the stitches as I knit – is an overhead effort with four arms each ending in an upturned pink glass lampshade with a black band round the bottom where dead flies have collected inside the shade. I could not bring myself to count the ornaments so I counted instead those I would put into the van if I were leaving like Mary and Vassily. The answer to this is three. The cracked glass vase; an unglazed pottery figure of a woman with a long skirt and a haughty expression, which is designed as a candle snuffer and therefore potentially of use but as there are no candles in the room it is no more useful than a vase that leaks; a wooden bowl, currently full of walnuts, two golf balls and a handful of loose change, which I would throw out before putting the bowl into the van. The vase was my mother's. I bought the candle snuffer on a holiday in Great Yarmouth. The bowl Edward bought for me at a country fair. It is not the associations, though, that lead me to choose these things. I choose them because I like to look at them.

I have occasionally railed against the quantity of objects in this house, and I know from his reaction that Edward's perception of them is different from mine. For him, the house represents continuity and tradition, security and roots. If he were turned out of the place tomorrow, even if he was left with a livelihood and somewhere else to live, he would be shivering like a man whose coat has been ripped off his back in a storm. He would feel exposed, insubstantial. For me, the house and all its contents are like the mud collecting on my boots as I walk the dog round the fields in a rainy season. Holding me back, weighting me down, limiting how far I can travel.

I am failing to be joyful in this letter. Please write and tell me what decisions you have taken about the objects in your house. Please tell me you have chosen to keep only those that give you pleasure. I am also worried about the position of your desk. I do not like to think of you facing a wall and writing to me. I would prefer to imagine you have a view of the clouds crossing the sky, of your neighbour's flagpole, a seagull or two. If there is nowhere else to put it, though, I would rather you wrote to me facing a wall than that you did not write to me at all.

Love,
Tina

Dear Tina,

You sound sad, in your letter, and I am sad that you are sad. Our correspondence began at a time when I was finding little reason to be happy, and it has brought me happiness. It would distress me greatly if it was making you unhappy. I mean, if it is causing you to think about your life in ways that make it seem a burden to you. You have lifted a burden of grief from me. I wish I could do the same for you. I worry that, as I have become more joyful, you may start to compare my chances for growing in happiness with your own, and this may cause you pain.

Let me tell you what I think now I have read your description of the room where you sit with your family. I think I would hate to be surrounded by all the things you say are in the room. I am not used to it and I admit I might find myself trying to group them together, to catalogue them. This would be necessary for me because it is my way of working. It is how I manage myself. I also think, though, there is evidence that people live in your house. They go in and out. They do what anyone might do in a house where they are at home. Change their bootlaces; read a manual; empty their pockets looking for a penknife, it might be. In my house, there is no one. When I return home from work, no lights are on, nothing has been touched since I left in the morning. I can understand the way you say your husband would feel if he were deprived of his home. I am often aware of the empty space behind me. Empty of movement, I mean. It is empty of ornament but I choose that it should be. I am more aware of the empty space because I have had it filled by my children this weekend, as well as because of your letters, which open another way of living to put alongside my own.

I will tell you about the weekend. I will not disguise how much I enjoyed it, even though this might appear unkind when you have nothing joyful to tell me. I know you will not think it unkind.

I cooked a stew, following a recipe from a book already on the shelf, making sure to do exactly as it said, down to measuring the quarter teaspoonful of salt. As it cooked, the smell filled the empty spaces, made them seem already like a home with people living in it. Erik and Karin arrived together on Friday night. I do not know the words (in English or Danish) to describe the lift in my heart when I opened the door and they were there. It was dark outside and they were lit up by the porch light, warm and solid and laughing at me in my apron covered in tomato pips and gravy. Karin is magnificent. She is fragile yet firm, weighted. She had draped herself in a knitted garment, a poncho I suppose it might be called, instead of a coat, and it wrapped itself round her body, hung in folds elegantly round her shoulders and over the mound that is my grandchild, her face rising up through the neck, just as beautiful (at least to me) as always, but with an added . . . now I have run out of words; what do I mean? Healthiness, shine, fulfilment? Something that was not there before.

I am sorry if I seem to be talking about my daughter as though she were the most special person in the world, when she is special only to me. But she is so special to me, at this time, waiting for the child to be born, and with the sunlight breaking through again after the misery of her mother's death. Of her mother's life, I could say. So much is said of post-traumatic stress. When I look at Karin now, I wonder if I am suffering from post-traumatic joy.

Erik is taller than either of us, but he is a man of passions, much more obvious passions than I am, and one of his passions is food, so he is plump. He is passionate about people, too. Kisses and hugs more than Karin or I do, than Birgitt did (she was particularly sparing with hugs). He laughs and cries much more easily. He is a delight to be with, but not restful.

Karin brought with her a loaf of bread with nuts and seeds in it, and a pudding she had made with apples. Erik brought a very fine bottle of red Burgundy wine, and these additions made the stew, which I believe was no better than ordinary, appear delicious. I had decorated the table with white porcelain plates and dishes, my loveliest simple glasses on slender stems, white linen napkins and three pewter candlesticks. (Your pottery lady who is also a candle snuffer would have a welcome place in my house.) We ate the food and Erik and I drank the wine. Karin has read all the latest books on pregnancy and would not taste it. Then we sat on the sofa, in front of the stove, and talked. Mostly we talked of Karin, her health and mood and the baby. The baby, she decided to tell me, when we were all together like this in the warmth with a

Bruch violin concerto playing softly, is a girl. She will be called Birgitt. I could not help feeling a little guilty that I could not stop myself being pleased, at this moment, that Karin has no husband, that the father of the child is on the other side of the world and ignorant of his daughter's existence. She will be born into my family, into the family that is Erik, Karin and me, and no one else will have as much right as us to love and nurture her. This is selfish, I know.

On Saturday morning, as we sat at breakfast, I told them I was wondering whether the display of objects I listed in my last letter should be allowed to stay as they are, unaltered, a monument to the strange obsessions of their mother's mind. Or was it time to look at them as if they had that moment been put down by an anonymous hand, and I could keep or dispose of them as I wished? According to whether I liked them or not. Erik folded his arms on the table and laid his head on them. I did not know what this response meant, so I looked at Karin, and she was smiling.

'Is this a good idea?' I said.

'It is a very good idea,' Karin said.

'Hallelujah!' said Erik, lifting his head from the table. 'I can't believe it has taken you so long.'

We lined up all the objects. I chose the piece of porcelain and the piece of wood shaped like an arch. These are things I like to look at. Karin chose the buttons and the pebbles. She has a friend who creates jewellery and sculptures from *objets trouvés* – so Karin called them. I expect you understand. Erik picked the slice of tree trunk. It is something, he says, that can fit on his desk, not in the way but not entirely out of sight, and it will recall his mother to him when his eye lights on it and he has nothing else in his mind, or only thoughts that he does not want to keep on thinking. This left us with the padlock, the bowl, the box, the fan and the nest of twigs. We put all these into a bag and Erik and I put on our coats and Karin wrapped herself up in her poncho; it is cold here, the wind is reminding us of winter.

We went into Silkeborg to a shop that buys and sells antiques. It sells nothing very large or very fine; in fact, much of what it offers is just old – is that different from antique? – and not very lovely or desirable. But I enjoy looking, and it sells books I sometimes buy, so I often visit. We offered the woman who runs it the box, the bowl and the fan. The shop is well lit but where the woman sits at the back, in an alcove behind a table covered with papers, it is very gloomy. I have never really looked at her but I had the impression of someone quite old. When we gave her the box made of playing cards and the fan, she switched on a bright lamp and I saw that in fact she is not exactly young, but not old at all. She has scars on her face, the sort of scars I imagine would be caused by injuries from a car accident. When she spoke to us about the items we had brought, it was obvious she is not Danish, though she speaks Danish. Here is someone else with a story to tell which I will never hear, I thought.

The fan, she said, was too damaged to be worth anything, but she liked the box and offered us money for it. Erik said at once we would not take the money but we would look for something in the shop to put in the empty spaces we had made by removing the fan and the box, and she might give us a discount on whatever we chose, if she liked. We looked through everything on all the shelves and tables and window-sills and at last we came across a piece of glass and I decided that was what I wanted. I may have had in mind the vase you talk of, though I have no idea what it looks like, what shape it is, what shade of green. Erik and Karin liked the piece of glass too, without having the connection to make. What we bought is shaped like a bottle with dimples (I think that is the right word) in the sides as if someone had pressed their thumb into it as it cooled. It is blue. It is not old, the woman who runs the shop told us, and it is chipped on the base and there is a tiny crack on the rim. It is in the shop, she said, because she liked it; the shape, the colour and the substance of it. She used a word in Danish which means solid strength, as a piece of wood might be solid and strong. It is not a word a native speaker might have used in this context, but a good one. She would take no money for the glass, only for the embroidered sampler that Karin bought for the wall of the baby's room. Worked by a girl called Alice who was twelve years old in 1905.

The shopkeeper did not want the bowl from an animal's hoof. It was too ugly, she said, and she was right. As we were about to leave, Erik brought out the padlock and offered it to her. If she had a use for it, he said, she was welcome to keep it. She said she had no fear of having things stolen, in Denmark, but there might come a time when she would wish to keep something safe, and she would be pleased to have the padlock, in case that time came.

When we left the shop we walked down to the lake. The surface was grey and ruffled in the wind, as it often is. Erik knelt down at the water's edge and Karin handed him the fan. He let it slide into the water, giving it a push to move it away from the shore. For a while it floated, but then the little waves raised by the breeze lapped over the tattered silk and overwhelmed the lacquered spokes, and it danced a little then sank out of sight. Next she passed him the bowl. He floated it across the surface and stood up with a handful of pebbles ready to sink it if it stayed afloat for too long, but it turned round twice in the water then plunged below the surface, all at once. I hope the hoof has not been treated in some way that will prevent it decaying, as all animal matter should decay, back into the mud.

Lastly Erik laid the nest of twigs on the water of the lake and we watched as the waves and the breeze played games with it, tossing it away from us then towards us as if inviting us to decide we did not really want to let it go. It looked so slight, as insignificant as any twig or leaf stripped from a tree in a storm. I could not believe I had kept it so carefully, for so long. At last it broke apart and went back to being just scraps – from any bush, it might be, any tree. Returning to the state it would have fallen into years ago if a human hand had not lifted it up from the earth and carried it away. As an archaeologist it is my job to pick things up from the earth and carry them away. Watching the twigs floating off to become part of all the other plant matter in the lake, I wondered whether it is a worthwhile way to spend a life. At least what you do produces food. How does what I do benefit anyone? I put these thoughts in here as part of the conversation I am having with you. They did not make me sad, standing on the bank with my beautiful, pregnant daughter and my plump and cheerful son. They do not make me sad now, writing them down for you. But I would be interested in what you might have to say on the subject.

Now the children have left and I am sitting at my desk, looking at the new empty spaces and the new piece of glass, and the darkness beyond the window, which would all have been behind me, until I moved my desk as you said I should.

Please do not be angry with the circumstances of your life. As your daughter said, nothing is so fixed it cannot be altered.

Love,
Anders

Bury St Edmunds
6th October

Dear Anders,

I do not know how I would cope without your letters. You make me ashamed of myself and yet happier. I am happier just knowing your desk is now facing the sky – our sky; your Scandinavian, my East Anglian sky. Your description of your children and how they make you feel was a joy to me and made me feel I should look more closely at my children, who I see every day without thinking about them at all. I should take more pleasure in who they are. I passed Tam in the yard, talking to an oil tanker driver who was making a delivery, and paused to look at him. He is built like his father, strong and square. He has his father's stance, too, slightly tilted as if he is expecting to move away any moment, or is leaning on a notional stick. He noticed me watching him and asked if there was anything I wanted. I could have said: 'I want to know you better,' but in fact I do know him, so perhaps I could have said: 'I want to feel closer to you.' I'm not sure how to achieve that.

I went into the machinery shed where Andrew was servicing the engine of the old tractor we keep for odd jobs, and because

Andrew likes old tractors and Edward does not like to get rid of anything until it is of no further use. Andrew is physically more like me, narrower, leaner, longer-legged than his brother. I asked if he was happy. We have a phrase: 'Are you happy in your work?' Which just means, do you need anything at the moment; is there anything I can do to help, that sort of thing. Andrew replied as if this was the phrase he had heard me say, rather than the question I meant to ask.

'I'd be happier if the light was better here,' he said. There is a strip light in the shed and he had an inspection lamp fixed up over the tractor, but I know what he meant because when I am sewing, the light is never quite good enough.

'Is that all it would take to make you happy?' I said. 'More light.'

He stopped what he was doing and looked at me slightly puzzled, slightly anxious.

'What's brought this on?' he said. 'Is something bothering you?'

'I was talking about you, dear,' I said. 'Not me. I'm happy enough.'

He looked relieved. 'That's good,' he said. 'So am I.'

I'm not sure either of us was telling the truth.

Now, the challenge: is archaeology a worthwhile occupation? It depends, I would say (avoiding rushing in with a strong opinion – this is right, this is wrong – as always), on how you define worthwhile. Now we have the basic requirements for survival – we have food and shelter and have a statistically tiny chance of being in danger of our lives – we might as well occupy ourselves with what is enjoyable or what is interesting. With the acquisition of knowledge. With ways of having fun. Don't you agree? If worthwhile means 'life-supporting', farming is better than archaeology. So is medical science. But if worthwhile is life-enhancing, well, anything that takes your fancy would be as worthwhile as the boring, simple business of producing food. Archaeology must have taken your fancy once.

We have been talking to each other about where life went, and if the way we each spent it was the way we meant to have spent it or would have chosen to spend it if we had known when we made our choices what the other choices were, but we have not wasted our lives. I insist on that.

Mary and Vassily have gone. They held their farewell party in one of the barns, and there were dozens and dozens of young people, some of them with children, dancing to the music provided by a group of musicians, some Lithuanian, some not. As you know, I am no judge of the quality of the music but it sounded tuneful to me and it filled the yard with sound. Vassily had fixed fairy lights all round the barn and the yard but the light they gave was ornamental rather than useful and it was hard to pick out who was who in amongst all the bodies moving about and talking, hard to recognise my own grand-children in amongst the flocks of children running back and forth. I kept close to the food at first; I felt responsible for making sure it was enjoyable to eat and although I couldn't influence anyone's enjoyment, or lack of it, at least I could tell from their behaviour if I had met my obligations. When the food had mostly been eaten, I set out to find Edward. He had not wanted the party to be in the barn, had not wanted the two of them to be leaving at all, and I was anxious, as the beer was being drunk, about what his mood might be. I was still looking for him when I met Sarah, my daughter-in-law, holding my two grandchildren, Amos and Zoe, by the hand. She asked if I would mind taking them home to bed, and staying with them, until she and Tam came home.

'We won't be late,' she said, but I could tell, from the colour in her cheeks and the way she walked, that she had already had enough to drink to make the party seem like the most fun in the world and therefore hard to leave.

Amos, Zoe and I went down the track to their bungalow, moving away from the music until only the deep beat of the bass could be picked out. Beyond the reach of the fairy lights, the sky was particularly clear, like a child's drawing of the night sky, crescent moon, stars and an inky darkness. I carried Zoe for the last hundred yards and she was asleep by the time we reached their home. I read Amos a story and he bounced on his bed the whole time, not listening, alive with excitement from the music, the games, the people, then went to sleep almost between one bounce and the next, one sentence and the next. I stayed awake until Tam and Sarah came home, long after midnight, mostly sitting in the dark, listening to the boom of the party. I find it hard to relax in that house. It was where my parents-in-law lived, I think I told you, and I hated it then for the resentment it harboured in its every brick and timber; they never wanted to move from the farmhouse and I was not an adequate reason for their eviction. Under Sarah's rule, it has been transformed into any suburban home, but it is not in a suburb and it makes me feel misplaced.

Edward was already in bed when I reached home, but not asleep. I had been wrong to worry about how he might behave as the party went on. The drink had made him happy and the flight from home of his only daughter was making him sad, so he was in a confused and loving state.

Now all that is behind us. They are gone and the mess from the party tidied up. The cottage where Vassily and Mary lived is empty and I have begun to prepare it for guests. I went again to the parlour and selected half a dozen pieces of furniture and objects I did not want in the room, and took them to the cottage. There, I washed, cleaned and polished them and put them in place, and when I stood back to look at what I had achieved, I was surprised to find that a wooden chair with a tapestry seat, a picture of some cows under a tree, an occasional table with curved legs and a leather top, a porcelain figure of a shepherdess and two red, cut-glass wine glasses all looked perfectly pleasant in their new home with their newly applied sparkle. I would never buy any of these things, in the shop you describe with the young-old lady in the alcove at the back, but they are not as hideous as I have always believed.

Of course, no one has noticed they have gone from the parlour.

Inspired by the Rag Man's gift of a dishcloth to someone who had let themselves sink into squalor, I also took down and washed the pink glass shades from the light fixture in the parlour, emptying out the dead flies of summers past. It is astonishing how uplifting this proved to be, though the light levels are now only slightly better and the fitting and shades as ugly as ever they were.

No one has noticed this improvement, either.

Edward is in a better mood, now the worst has happened and they are gone. Here is Daphne installed in the farm office a couple of days a week, looking busy, and here am I with a tidier, cleaner, less cluttered parlour and a spruced-up holiday cottage. So all is well.

I can see that living alone, as you do, leaves empty space around you, and that can feel lonely. Living together with other people, as I do, can feel lonely, too.

Love,
Tina

Copenhagen
16th October

Dear Tina,

You will see from the address that I am with Karin in Copenhagen. Since last I wrote, when I was full of such pride, I have fallen into a sort of despair. Nothing is very wrong, I must tell you at once, so do not fear to read on.

Karin slipped on a step and damaged her ankle, not badly, but they took her into hospital and decided everything was not quite as it should be. Her blood pressure and so on. She must, they told her, rest completely or there is a risk to her and to the baby. So I have come here to look after her and to make sure she does nothing. This is not easy. She knows she should not move, so she lies on the sofa and I bring her coffee and cake, and soup and sandwiches, during the day, and something warm and tasty for the evening meal. I do not have to cook any of these, as there are friends who come every day, always with something in a tin or a dish or a saucepan for me to serve to Karin whenever she needs food. However, it is the friends that make the task of looking after Karin difficult. (Is that sentence correct? Can I use the singular 'is' with the plural 'friends'? I am improving my English by checking words and structures as I write to you, but this looks wrong.) The friends bring cheerfulness and chatter into the flat, and they bring things with them that are not food to eat – opinions, news, books, DVDs, flowers. All of these things stir Karin up and she becomes excited and lively, talking to her friends and pointing out where to put the flowers, or telling them what her opinions are, what books she has read. It makes me feel tired just to be in the room with them all, so I go into the kitchen or, if that is also full, out onto the streets to walk or cycle round the neighbourhood in the cold. I understand now, that loneliness is worse if there are people about than if there are not.

Karin says the friends do not tire her; they keep her from thinking about her health and the baby's health and what is to come. Her colleagues from work come, too, and bring files. 'That is not doing nothing,' I told Karin when I found her reading one. This time she agreed, and laid it aside. She has begun to talk of Ben again, the baby's father. She says that this warning from the doctors has made her wonder if, after all, she should let him know about baby Birgitt. What if something happens to her, and she is not able to look after the child, or is not here to look after her? I can say nothing to this. I cannot say 'I am here' because I know I am not the answer. I am the wrong person to be given the task of bringing up a baby. Not just because I am a man, and no longer young, without a wife, but because I have not the skill of showing love, obviously, openly and constantly, as a baby has a right to expect. I do not know if Ben has this skill. I have seen a photo of him. He looks sturdy (I have searched my thesaurus for the right word and I think this is it), but what else can I tell about him?

So I am here, on an edge, is how I feel. I do not know if Karin will carry this baby through the next ten weeks and give birth to her, safely. If the baby will be born perfect. If the baby will be shared with an unknown father. I feel as if I am waiting for something to happen. All my married life I was waiting for something to happen and hoping it never would. Now I am hoping for something to happen and fearing it never will.

Write to me.

Love,

Anders

Bury St Edmunds
20th October

My dear Anders,

If you look at the people walking, driving or cycling past you as you go round the part of Copenhagen where Karin lives, you should think: every one of these was once an unborn child; every one of them has been born and survived childhood and has, most probably, children of their own. Pregnancy and childbirth are overwhelming when they happen to you or to those close to you, but they are normal. I will regret having written this if something happens which means for Karin and baby Birgitt it is not normal, but it is unlikely the news you give me when next you write will be anything other than good. But just in case, I will make you a promise. If the news is bad, if the unlooked-for worst should happen, I will at last visit the museum at Silkeborg and we can stand side by side in front of the Tollund Man and accept that our lives are part of a sequence which has endured and will endure and our own sorrows and joys are important only to us. Having made this promise, I am for the first time able to say, I hope I do not have reason to visit Silkeborg soon.

I am the wrong person to ask about grammar; I just power along stringing words together and if they make sense, I am happy. If they make sense to you, that is all that matters. What you say makes sense to me and I like the way you say it. Please keep writing, just as you have been doing.

I am hoping for good news about Karin and baby Birgitt.

Love,

Tina

Silkeborg
30th October

Dear Tina,

You are right. Childbirth is commonplace. Karin is better now; there is no longer any risk to the baby and her ankle is improving. She is working from home for the next two weeks and will then stop until after the baby is born. Her doctor, her midwife and her friends have all told her this is the right plan, and she has agreed. I think it is the right plan as well, of course, but I do not think my opinion, if it was not backed up by the others, would have counted. I have come home. I was necessary at first, then I became unnecessary. I was stopping Karin from leading her life as she normally would, by being there, so now I am here, and back at work myself.

I have a commission to write a book about fertility goddess figures, which is timely, as I am thinking so much about fertility and the need for good luck, which, in the Bronze and Iron Ages, meant a good god who would give you the gift of healthy children. This book is not for scholars – which would require more study and field visits than I am inclined to carry out – but for whomever may have an interest. Of course this still means it has to be accurate, as far as facts are concerned, and where there are no facts, I have to have good reasons for my speculations, and balance my speculations with the speculations of others. So there is much work to be done. I have, you will not be surprised to know, developed a way of grouping the figures, a sort of catalogue. This is work I can do while sitting in my own office, and I am enjoying the task.

I am worried that, having helped each other overcome sorrow, we are sinking ourselves deeper in hopelessness. Helplessness. I look up, now, from my desk at home and I can see the sky, which today is the sort of blue that is very deep, softened by a film of white. As if it is a strong colour that has chosen to be muted and restful. I can see my neighbour's flagpole and the rope hanging alongside it, not moving. How did you know my neighbour had a flagpole? Did I mention it to you? It is a very Danish thing, I think. Nearer to me than the window or the sky are the piece of shaped wood, the piece of pottery and the blue glass with dimples. (I know you do not want to correct my grammar, but if ever I use a word that is wrong, you must tell me.) The light coming through the window illuminates the top of each of these objects, but the part nearest me is in shade, the shapes merging into the white surface of the piece of furniture. I cannot feel hopeless or helpless as long as I am sitting here, looking at these things, writing to you.

I have left it until last to say something about your promise. I do not want you to have to come to comfort me for a loss. Although, if I were to suffer a loss, your coming would be the only comfort I would be able to imagine. I want you to come when you have your own need to come, not because I need you. I do not know when that will be. I do not know why that will be. I will wait.

Love,
Anders

Bury St Edmunds
12th November

Dear Anders,

I am pleased all is well with Karin. That is enough to raise my spirits, even without the sky and the ornaments and the flagpole (which you did mention to me in an earlier letter). I am looking at the sky, too, and it is grey and every so often a rook is swept past, or more probably flies past, but it always looks as if they have no say in the matter, but are lifted and carried by the wind like so many bundles of feathers. I am excited, too, about your book.

My life has no drama. Now Mary and Vassily have gone, we are all jogging on in our usual way, except Gregor is up a ladder fixing the guttering, rather than Vassily, and Daphne is in the office, not Mary. I am spending more time than usual in the office with Daphne. This is partly because it is the warmest place to be. There are two gas heaters and Daphne has them turned up full, all day. I am expecting ructions when the cylinders of gas run out and more have to be ordered.

Mary was less prodigal with the heat and would eke out one cylinder per heater for the whole winter, but Daphne is less hardy a beast and I don't see why I should begrudge her the warmth. I notice Edward making more visits to the office than he used to do. He likes to warm himself up as much as the next man, and so I shall remind him when more gas is needed.

I am also spending time in the office making sure Daphne is doing the job properly. I am no expert on figures but I do understand the business of farming – the debits and the credits of it – and I can often spot mistakes she makes, it seems to me, because she does not pay attention to what she is doing. I hope, if I keep pointing these out to her, she will over time become either better at noticing them or more diligent in avoiding them, or both. Although it is actually possible that she makes more mistakes because I am in the office with her. It means she has someone to talk to and talking is what she enjoys. It is quite hard for me because I only enjoy talking when I have a topic I want to talk about to someone whose reaction I am interested in. I am talking to you all the time, for example, only as words on the page, but if we were face to face, I am sure I would find it as easy to chatter on about music and poetry and joy and grief as it is to do this on paper. I do not know how to take part in Daphne's conversation, however, and I do not want to take part in it.

Daphne's favourite topic is the failings of other people. It has taken me a little while to notice this as she has a smiling, humorous way of talking, starting off with a laugh and a phrase expressing amusement or disbelief, such as: 'Honestly, would you credit . . .' or 'You'll never believe this . . .' When she has finished telling me what she set out to tell me, she will end with a phrase expressing good will and tolerance, such as: 'That's life, I suppose' or 'Well, she probably can't help it', and she will laugh again, as if she is endlessly amused by the world even while it is frustrating her.

She was telling me this morning about catching her mother's carer drying the dishes with a roll of kitchen paper, instead of a tea towel. ('I mean, kitchen roll!') The woman said she thought it was more hygienic to use paper and throw it away than spread germs about with a dirty cloth. ('I ask you, what does she think washing machines are for!') The carer is a fruitful object for such stories, and so is her mother, who – would you believe it? – asks for something one day and then can't remember why she wanted it the next. But she is ready to throw in anecdotes about the ridiculous opinions or behaviour of almost anyone and chats away about Lorna and Margaret and Judy when I really have no idea who these people are. All I know is, they are always saying or doing things Daphne would never dream of saying or doing, can you believe it?

I have sat beside Daphne at parties, when her husband was still alive, in the company of other women – they might have been Lorna or Margaret or Judy – and they have been able to react with suitable outrage or laughter or humorous tolerance to the things Daphne says, and then to throw in some examples of their own. I have never been able to do this. I could tell her my opinion: for instance, that I can see the carer has a point and using kitchen paper to wipe the dishes dry is a sensible idea; that her mother is nearly ninety and should be allowed to let her mind wander. And sometimes I do this, and she looks at me as if I have failed to see the joke, so most of the time I smile when she does, and let her think I agree with her, caught out by my own inability to face conflict.

Now, of course, I realise that I am doing exactly what I am criticising someone else for doing. I have complained at length about the failings of Daphne Trigg – that is, her lack of capacity to understand and empathise with the failings of others and her failure to find any topic of conversation except the failings of others. And what am I doing in this letter, then? I am ashamed of myself, but it is also making me smile.

As the winter goes on I will grow used to the cold and Daphne will grow used to the books and I will stop going into the office and go back to doing the other things that fill my days: caring for the hens, cooking, cleaning, walking the dog, lending a hand whenever and wherever a hand is needed. This will be better for my peace of mind, and my character. I am planning to visit Mary and Vassily soon and I am looking forward to travelling to meet them, and to the mountains, but also to having some other, less pedestrian topic to talk to you about.

Love,
Tina

Silkeborg
20th November

Dear Tina,

I need you to keep telling me what you are doing and think-ing. It has become important to me to have a connection with a life that is not mine, for I feel boxed up within my own life at this time.

I remember you told me, at the beginning, that yours was a buried life. I feel so it is, now, with mine. I am working on the book and while I am digging up facts about figures dug up from the earth, I am also burying myself in their form and meaning. So much of this meaning is about wombs and childbirth, and while I concentrate on the screen, I am all the time waiting for the telephone to ring. Inside the space I occupy, physically, all is calm. There are no shocks, only the patient uncovering of facts, the business of relating those facts to other facts. Outside the space I occupy is all the uncertainty of childbirth. The figures I look at on the screen and handle at the museum are hard; Karin, in the image I hold in my head, is so soft, and softness cannot resist damage as hardness can. I am finding it difficult to reconcile these things in my mind as I work.

The earliest of the fertility figures were no more than an upright shape, no breasts, no broad hips or big stomach. They can be identified as a representation of a woman only by the carving of a necklace round where the throat would be. This is also confusing me. I do not know whether to be comforted by the simplicity or angry at the simplification.

You see, I need your letters to help me make sense of the world.

I am thinking, as well, about becoming a grandfather and remembering, as a consequence, my own grandfather, my father's father, that is (I never knew my mother's father). He stands in my mind as the symbol for all grandfathers, as the goddess figures stand for all women. He is as far from the real grandfather I am about to become as the figure I have on the screen at the moment is from Karin. He was a man who was aloof and austere (I have looked these words up, I hope you like them) and I admired him greatly, from what I knew of him and from the stories told about him.

My grandfather was a farmer, during the war. You must know that Denmark was occupied in 1940; at first the government cooperated with the Germans to preserve some neutrality, but it meant that almost everything the farm produced would have been shipped to Germany to feed the population, and times were quite hard here in Denmark. We are not a people who easily become subjects, I believe, and from the start there was resistance and sabotage. I do not know if my grandfather took part in this; he never spoke of the war.

In 1943, things changed and both the resistance activities and the control of the Germans increased. At this time, they issued an order to round up all the Jews and deport them to concentration camps. Before this could happen, almost all of them ran away from their homes and, with the help of the resistance and the Danish people, were evacuated to Sweden. My grandfather's farm was near the coast and he played a part in this evacuation by sheltering Jewish families as they waited for boats to carry them to safety. One night some Germans turned up at the farm; they had been patrolling the coastal area and found they had not enough fuel to reach their base. There was a Jewish family staying in the house: mother, father and a child about three years old. My grandfather went out to the Germans and led them off to the barn where the fuel for the tractor was stored; my father, who was a teenager, went with them. But the little Jewish boy, not understanding the danger, escaped from his mother and ran out after them, into the barn where the four men – two Germans, my father and grandfather – were busy with the oil drum.

At once, my grandfather picked the child up and began

playing games with him, tickling him and swinging him over his head, making him laugh, to stop him saying anything that might give them away.

'This is your son?' said one of the Germans, and my grandfather said no, it was the son of his brother, who lived with them now, since his father had been killed fighting for the Germans as part of the volunteer brigade, the Freikorps Danmark (which was of course despised by my grandfather and his family). All the time spinning the little boy about to stop him talking, while my father filled the container with fuel for the Germans' car. At last it was ready, and my father carried it to the car for them, diverting them from the house. They gave him money, when they left, a tip, I suppose, and said what a fine young man he was. They gave a coin, too, to the little Jewish boy, for being the son of someone who had fought on their side. The way the story was told afterwards, by the rest of the family but never by my grandfather himself, my grandfather carried the child back to the house and picked up the piece of bread he had been eating when the Germans arrived, as if nothing had happened.

When I was a child I used to pretend to myself that I was the little boy my grandfather had played with; he was so calm, so remote, so grand a figure to me it seemed a miraculous thing that he might play with me in this way. When my father grew old and bitter he would tell the story again, complaining about the fear he felt at the time, and how his father had cared more for the safety of the fugitive family than he had for his own wife and children. At his worst, he would say how unfair it was, that his father, who had never played with his own children, should have just this once shown such playfulness to a stranger's child.

I cannot imagine that Karin's daughter will have any such stories to tell of me, when she is my age. But I will try to be a person she thinks worth remembering. I am talking as if it is a certainty that Karin will have a daughter who will live to be my age, all the while listening for the ringing of the telephone.

Write soon.

Love,

Anders

Bury St Edmunds
7th December

My dear Anders,

Aloof and austere are good words. I like them. They do not apply to my own grandparents at all. The one I remember best is my mother's mother, who we called Nan. She was a gardener. Her husband, who I don't remember, was a market gardener – he grew vegetables for sale in the local shops and on his market stall – and she gardened alongside him, growing food to eat, but she also created a garden round their bungalow in Norfolk which was a wonder. There seemed to be no planning in it, and she never knew any of the proper names for the plants, never mind the names of the botanical families to which they belonged. Such things were of no importance to her. She could recognise the plants she grew and she had names for them that I think were often her own names that she chose to call them, rather than a label that would allow other people to know what they were. She put plants in where she wanted them to grow, and they grew. Or she put them in where there happened to be a space, and still they grew. It is her hands I remember most clearly. My mother didn't like us eating any of the food Nan prepared when we visited, because they had soil so deeply ingrained in every crevice they never looked clean. Her hands looked as if they had gripped things – tools, weeds, watering cans – for so many years they had formed into a permanent gripping shape, the knuckles raised in a ridge across the back and the fingertips worn away. She was always looking at what was close to her, right under her feet, under her trowel, or into the distance where the roses were in flower or the cherry trees fruiting; never into anyone's face.

There is a story of her, too, from wartime, which is often told in the family. The war never came near her – although there were air bases in East Anglia that were targeted, none was close to where she lived. But the district lost twelve young men, whose names are recorded now on the war memorial in the village. Each time news was brought of a death, she would plant something in memory of that young man, whether she knew him or not. She dug a hole on the verge beside the war memorial, which only had names from the First World War on it at the time, and planted whatever she had chosen, then marked the spot with a stick naming the person who had died. She asked no one if she could do this, although she had no right to be planting there, and she did not mention it to the families, but somehow everyone knew and no one minded. Some of the plants grew too big, over time, for the place where she had put them, and these have been moved to somewhere close, each still identified with the name of the person she was thinking of when she planted it. Or, if the plant was too big to move, cuttings were taken. Some of the plants are not long-lived, and these too have been replaced with cuttings of the original or, if necessary, with a new plant of the same type. The families took cuttings too, over the years, and the plants growing round the war memorial in the village can be seen in many of the gardens round about. Girls who were the sisters or the nieces or cousins of the young men had pieces of the shrub commemorating their relative in their bouquets when they married. There are girls called Rose and Rosemary and Laurel in the area, in memory of men who died seventy years ago.

I owe my love of plants and gardens to Nan, but maybe also she is the original inspiration for my thoughts on the past and its links to the present, which is why I come to be writing this letter and, even more important, looking forward to the next letter from you.

Now, about your book. I am struck by the idea of the stick that represents a woman in a tangential way, without being whittled into a figure with a head, breasts, arms and legs. I like the subtlety of it; the carving is there as a suggestion, but the man or woman holding it or running a finger over it may invest it with his or her own meaning, which is probably inexpressible. It is a female, but female in any way the person who sees or touches it understands what femininity is. So it would be if I were to have a conversation with a neighbour about what it meant to be British. I know what it feels like, to me, but it is too complex to articulate and, if I could put it into words, my feeling would be different from (but not completely distinct from) my neighbour's. We could both hold the stick symbolising Britishness and think, as we touched it, Ah, yes, that's right, that's how it is, while the unarticulated ideas in our heads are both overlapping and diverging. So it must be for you, knowing what it is to be Danish. The later figures, with breasts and hips and stomachs, look like cruder symbols, a formalisation of woman as a means of reproduction, but in their very crudeness they have the scope to be more than they represent. They are exaggerated but incomplete; the gaps are there for whoever looks or touches to fill. I envy you the chance to look at and touch and draw meaning from these things. I can imagine these figures, being held, triggering thoughts going backwards, forwards, sideways.

Now here I am chuntering on about fertility goddesses as if I know something about the subject, when I know nothing. I only know what Professor Glob has written about and shown me in the pictures in his book. But I cannot help being excited at all you will find out, all you will record and catalogue; all the connections you will make between one figure and another, between the figures and the tribes who produced them. It is nearly Christmas (bear with me, this is relevant) and I am plucking and dressing turkeys and geese for the local butchers' shops and farm gate sales, so at this time of year it is my hands that are busy. When I am not putting food on the table, I am working in the poultry shed, often until late at night as the plucking and drawing come at the end of the process and the birds killed during the day have to be plucked while still warm. As I do this I think of you, with a desk lamp illuminating the pad on which you are taking notes, and the screen lit up with words and images in front of you; I see your fingers on the keyboard or picking up a pen; I imagine you pulling a book into the circle of light to check one fact or another, add a detail or two to what you have found out so far. And I look at my hands, red with cold and turkey viscera, and at the dead birds (or food for the table, depending on whether I choose to see what is before me as it was an hour ago or what it will become an hour from now) illuminated by the arc lights set up in the shed.

Now I expect you are expecting me to begin wailing about how life could have led me to this feather-and-down-filled shed when it delivered you up to a quiet, warm study? But, actually, there is a more complex relationship between my feelings and the two situations. I have never minded doing the turkeys and the geese. Each of them presents as a self-contained task and each of them, finished, represents the successful completion of a task. Preparing the Christmas birds is a family event; other people play Monopoly or charades, we kill, pluck and draw the guts out of poultry. We have relays of soup and sandwiches, coffee and cake. We have the radio tuned to a station playing Christmas songs and carols. We have a collective sense of achievement which is better than a triumph achieved alone: not only did I do this, and do it well, but I was successful in filling my place on the line, my part in the overall production. Despite this, of course, I cannot help but imagine how much I would enjoy the task of finding out facts and creating a story around those facts, alone, in silence. Maybe one day I will sit at a desk, sifting the information in front of me. Planning and creating rather than plucking and drawing. Like the mountains and the missed raspberries, I will look forward to when it might be so. Meanwhile, I will enjoy the thought that it is so for you, and through you I can imagine this other life which you are leading on my behalf.

Christmas is, as I said, a busy time. I will go to Inverness after it is all over, the food eaten and the drink drunk and the decorations, which look so cheerful and festive when they are first put up, have become so much debris to be cleared away. Maybe baby Birgitt will have been born by the time I leave. Then we will have two joyous letters. Mine about a journey. Yours about an arrival.

Much love,
Tina

Copenhagen
14th December

My Dear Friend,

If my English is not so good in this letter, I hope you will forgive me. I am so tired, but I need to write to you before I can sleep. It is become that I cannot understand myself properly unless I am talking to you.

The night before last I was eating my evening meal when the phone rang, just as I had feared it would. It was a friend of Karin's; his name is Jesper and he is married to Sofia. I think I have not spoken of them before. Karin had told me Sofia would be with her when the baby was born, so when he said, on the phone, 'It is Jesper,' I thought the baby had come. It is two weeks before the baby should come. That is not so serious, I thought. But Jesper said the baby was not come and it was serious. Karin was in the hospital, and the doctors were doing everything they could but Jesper did not know what that was. He did not know how serious it was. Sofia was with Karin, Jesper said.

I left the house at once, and got into my car and drove to Copenhagen. It takes three and a half hours to drive from

Silkeborg to Copenhagen. It was dark, of course, and there was nothing beyond the windscreen but, every so often, lights by the roadside, lights coming towards me. Mostly, it was just dark. I drove in silence the whole way, stopping only once to buy coffee and fuel. I could not listen to the radio because what point was there to anything that might be playing at that time, if Karin was going to be taken from me? I could hardly bear to look at the other people in the place where I stopped because what right had they to be alive if I was going to lose my daughter? The only thought that kept me from despair during those hours was that if she left me, you would come. I would not have to bear the grief alone.

When I reached the hospital it seemed impossible to park and impossible to find the part of the building where Karin was and then to find the right rooms in that part of the hospital. At last, I found Jesper. He was folded into a chair in a waiting area. He is a very tall young man, very thin. He started to stand up when he saw me and he did not speak to me until he was standing and it took him so long to straighten himself out but at last he was able to tell me that they – Karin, Sofia – were in the operating theatre and he was waiting for someone – Sofia, a nurse, a doctor – to come out and tell him what was happening.

We waited together. Jesper is not a man who chatters and neither am I, so we waited, mostly, in silence. We might even have looked calm, to anyone passing by. I had my briefcase with me. I had left it in my car when I returned home from work and it was still in my car when I arrived at the hospital so I picked it up and took it in with me. I do not know why. As we waited, I took out the feather from the wing of a female pheasant and held it in one hand, touched it with the other.

It is nothing like the fertility goddess figures I am writing about, except that it is strong. It is also soft, as women are and the figures are not. I took out your letter and read it again, starting with your thoughts on symbols and carrying on through the poultry shed. My mind was disturbed by the image of the plucked bodies of birds and at this moment, when the horror of what might be happening behind the doors in the corridor became more than I could physically bear, Sofia came through one of the doors and walked towards us.

She is a very pretty girl with curly hair and she was wearing earrings in the shape of little sea creatures. (I do not have my dictionary here so I cannot name them. They are *søhest* in Danish.) I could not look at her face as she came towards us because if it was bad news I would know at once but if I waited until she was close enough to tell us, it could be she would never reach us and I need never know. So I kept looking at the silver creature hanging from her left ear and, at last, she did reach us and she said: '*Alter i orden*', which means everything is all right.

Sofia and Jesper both stepped up to me and put their arms round me and, so, round each other, and all of us cried.

Later, I went in to see Karin and she was white – white, and very weak. But she smiled at me and asked me to go and see the baby, who is in a special place for babies who do not bounce into the world ready to live. If Karin had not asked I would not have gone to look at the baby, with images of dead birds still in my mind. But I went, and a nurse took me to meet my granddaughter for the first time and she was lying asleep, a little parcel of arms and legs and fingers and toes, and of course I remembered how it was to see Erik for the first time, how at once I knew I would stand between him and anything that might hurt him, because how could he not be precious to me?

The nurse told me little Birgitt is in no danger, is only in this place so Karin can rest.

'I thought I might be going to lose them both,' I told her.

'Ah, but you know,' she said, 'childbirth is so normal.'

'I know,' I said. 'A good friend said this to me but last night I could not quite believe her words.'

I went back to Karin's room and stayed with her for a while but she was asleep and also, so the nurse said, in no danger, so I came here to her flat and am writing all this to you before I try to sleep. When I went into the bathroom and looked in the mirror I did not recognise the man I am this morning. I have not shaved – I have not brought a razor – and my face looks like someone else's face. Like my father, who was a sour, disappointed man. In old age he drank too much and cared too little for himself or for the people round him. It was strange, when I feel so full of love and joy, to feel it might be his face looking back at me. If I closed my eyes, I thought, and covered my head with a leather cap, I might look as much like the Tollund Man as my father. But with my eyes shut I would never know if I did.

I am making no sense now and must sleep. Thank you for letting me share this with you.

Happy Christmas,
Your loving friend,
Anders

My dear Anders,

I am writing quickly. A short letter, in amongst the turmoil of Christmas. I am sorry I filled your mind with images of dead birds. I am filled with joy for you and for Karin.

Whenever babies arrive, to people close to me, I knit. It takes a few evenings to finish knitting things the size that babies wear. I could not knit for your granddaughter because it seemed too ordinary and too intimate. Instead, I am sending you a poem. This is from a book called *Newborn* by Kate Clanchy. It is one of the books the volunteer in the Oxfam bookshop saved for me (her name is Laura; having introduced her into our correspondence it felt discourteous not knowing what to call her. She was pleased to be asked. She did not know my name either and it seemed absurd, to both of us, when we had exchanged so much in the way of feelings and ideas). The poem I have chosen says what I would like to say to you about the whole business of the coming into the world of a new child, but I do not know how to say it.

What Can I Say
Like the Japanese tricks
you could buy for twopence
those tight lacquer seeds
which uncurled in water
then bloomed into red
tissue flowers, algal, alarming;
or those cellophane fish
that twitched on your palm
for 'fever' or 'lust'; like

those shit-coils of sand
a razor-fish shoots out
when it sink-drills itself
back to wet salt and you think
how can a shelled thing
be so fast and afraid: like
all things unfolding, tumbling,
suddenly, catkins, fishing nets,
mainsails, sheets, like
the reel's hectic spooling
when the salmon is hooked,
like a parachute abruptly
uncrushing, blooming
to skull-shape, jerking you
upright with that familiar crack;
this opening up of a person,
this bringing the new person out.

Of course, this is more intimate than a knitted hat or mittens. But it is intimate in a different way. The knitting says: I think I know what you like enough to know you will want your baby to wear this. The poem says: I think I know you well enough to know you understand how I feel.

Early in the New Year I am going to Inverness. I will write from there. If Karin wants something knitted, you must tell me.

All my love,
Tina

Copenhagen
20th December

Dear Tina,

I will write quickly, too. To say thank you for the poem. Karin also says thank you. I have read it carefully and slowly and cannot be sure yet that I understand it. Karin has understood it better than I have done and has asked a friend to find her the book. She also says, if you would like to knit something for the baby that is not pale pink she would be honoured to receive it.

We are all here in Karin's flat – Karin, Birgitt, Erik and myself. It is very warm in the flat and it seems very full with objects for the baby. A cradle, boxes of nappies, a baby bath, shawls and rattles and so on. Most of these are much bigger than the baby is. She is still very small and takes up little space but all of these objects and the three of us fill all the space there is.

I look at Birgitt and cannot believe that something so fragile can survive, but she is doing more than survive, she is growing and developing just as she should. (Karin has just looked over my shoulder to see what I am writing and tells me that this is exactly what the poem says. I will read it again.)

We, Erik and I, will leave tomorrow and I think that will be good. It will make room for Karin and Birgitt to work out a way of living together. I will write again from Silkeborg.

Love,
Anders

Inverness
8th January

My dear Anders,

Here we are, sailed safely into another year. Our families intact and nothing to be waiting for, with dread or hope. Let us hope that the year will bring no sorrow. Is that a suitable New Year's wish, do you think? Or am I wishing for nothing, only survival without pain, and is that worth wishing for? I didn't intend to start this letter this way. I don't know where these thoughts come from except that when I sit down to write to you it seems as if all the strings holding my conscious mind together come loose and let my sub-conscious leak out. I will recover myself and be blithe.

Here I am, in Inverness. I came by train. That was a joy in itself. The sequence of trains and stations was:

1. Bury St Edmunds to Peterborough
2. Peterborough to York
3. York to Inverness

I am putting in the detail because I believe you would like it and, because you like it, I like it, too. The first train was full; I had booked a seat but there was a young man already in it, fast asleep, and I did not like to wake him so I was prepared to stand until the next station, but then a girl stood up and offered me her seat. I rarely go anywhere by public transport so I was shocked to find I have slid over some line which marks out those young enough to stand from those who are owed the respect of the young and must be made to sit. I nearly refused but realised in time that would a) make me look like an old curmudgeon and b) rob her of the satisfaction of doing the right thing. So I accepted, with a smile. She smiled back and she had the sort of smile that is a pleasure to see.

I did a lot of fidgeting, on this first part of the journey, which was about an hour, trying to take my coat off, because I was too hot, and to unscrew the lid of my thermos flask, which might have become a little rusty from lack of use. I was irritating the man with a laptop sitting next to me and, what with this and not being comfortable, I wished I had remained standing. But then I would have missed the girl's lovely smile.

At Peterborough I had to clutch all my belongings and scamper to another platform to catch the train to York. This time I sat in my booked seat. I sorted myself out before I sat down and began to enjoy myself. I wanted the train to go a little slower, though, so I could have more time to speculate about the people living in the houses we went past, the people waiting on the platforms, walking their dogs, picking sprouts in their allotments. As well as watching all this happening through the window, I was listening to the voices in the carriage with me. As the train came closer to York, more and more of these had Yorkshire accents and I love to hear people speaking in accents I do not often come across; the same words but set to a new tune which sounds more lyrical, more interesting, more cheerful than the tune I usually hear. Altogether I enjoyed myself so much I forgot to eat my lunch.

At York, which is a beautiful station, I had to scamper again to catch the train to Inverness. This time my seat was at a table, two people facing me, one beside me. I settled in and ate my sandwiches, then, because there was nothing but countryside outside the window – and I am too used to countryside for it to be exciting – I started knitting for baby Birgitt. It takes over six hours to travel from York to Inverness, not quite enough time to finish what I started, but I will send it in my next letter. It is a little bear, which I have knitted in moss stitch, wearing a blue jumper in stocking stitch. This will mean nothing to you, but moss stitch is knobbly, stocking stitch smooth, so two different textures for the baby to feel. And more interesting to knit than using just the one stitch.

There was a man sitting next to me, a woman opposite me and a man beside her. They all watched me knitting. I noticed this because, when I was just an ordinary no-longer-young, undistinguished sort of woman eating her beef sandwiches and an apple, I could tell I was close to invisible. They had other things to look at and think about. If I had left the train at the next stop they would not have been able to recall a single feature of my appearance by the time the train pulled out of the station. But as I began to cast on, they became alert to my existence. I knitted a few rows and, looking up for a moment, caught the eye of the woman opposite.

'What are you knitting?' she asked.

'A teddy bear for a friend's first grandchild,' I said.

'My grandmother knitted me a beautiful dress, in a Fair Isle pattern,' she said. 'I was only about five, but I can remember it so well. When I had my children, I tried to learn but I never got the hang of it.'

'I can knit,' said the man sitting next to me. 'Not Fair Isle or anything complicated, but I can knit.'

So we talked about knitting. The man opposite said no one in his family had ever knitted, and he sounded quite despondent as he said this, in contrast to the man beside me who was positively proud of having finished two scarves, while his sisters had fallen at the hurdle of making a square.

The woman had tripped over the same milestone and had given up when every square turned out, on completion, to be a rhomboid instead. The man who knitted admitted he had started a pair of mittens, never finished. He was sure his mother would have kept them; next time he saw her, he would ask, and maybe take them up again and, this time, finish them. The woman had a friend who knitted and thought she might make a last effort to learn from her. The man who had never knitted remembered a friend of his wife who had knitted a whole jumper using a technique called *entrelac*, which he understood was tricky to do. They all looked at me. Very tricky, I said.

They began to be interested in the detail of what I was doing. I explained the stitches, and the approach to the construction (the bear will be sewn together rather than knitted in the round), the type of wool, the pattern. The pattern was particularly enthralling because they could not understand how I was able to translate the random numbers and letters on the page into a set of instructions. Like reading music, I said. Which I can't do, but if I could, and I could play an instrument, which I also can't do, I would see at once what a page of notes was instructing me to produce in the way of a tune.

Then the woman began to talk about her grandmother who had made the never-to-be-forgotten Fair Isle dress, and how she missed her. The man who never knitted had, as it happened, just lost his grandmother; she had been a woman it was hard to like but he found he missed her too, unexpectedly, if only because he had become so used to wondering what she would object to in his clothes, friends, occupation, topics of conversation, when next they met. Now he found he was becoming more critical of all these things himself, as if he didn't have to bother while she did the job for him. The man who knitted had a grandmother who used to fly the Spitfires from the factory to the airfields in the Second World War.

When the topic of grandmothers was exhausted, the woman asked me about the baby whose toy this was going to be. I had never seen her, I said. She lived in Denmark. I had never visited Denmark. Only the man who didn't knit had been to Denmark and he had spent a year there. His knowledge of Denmark compensated for his lack of knowledge of knitting; at least I hope he thought it did.

The others, who had not been to Denmark either, became convinced that they should go. By the time we reached Edinburgh, where they all left the train, they were certain they would be going, and soon. To hear them talk so easily of making the journey brought back the feelings of frustration that made me write to Professor Glob in the first place. Never to have been to Silkeborg. Despite having intended to since I was more than two decades younger than the woman sitting opposite me. I realised that writing to you has become a way of visiting the Tollund Man without visiting him. Maybe I am frightened to do it. Have always been frightened and am more frightened now.

After Edinburgh it was dark and the train stopped again and again at places that sprang up, brightly lit, out of the darkness, and then vanished again behind us. I knitted on until I became weary and then sat, doing nothing, and thinking nothing until the train arrived in Inverness and there was my lovely Mary, a slender pillar of calm in the hubbub.

I have had to wait until now, when it is daylight, to see the mountains. You are right, it is important to see mountains from time to time. They are so much more than it is possible to remember. Journeys to loved ones, too. You were right about that. I am at least starting the year by doing something I have never done before. Perhaps that should be my New Year's wish. That I should carry on doing things I have never done before.

I will write again soon, and send the bear.

All my love,

Tina

Silkeborg
9th January

Dear Tina,

I begin to feel I can hear your voice, when I read your writing. I almost believe I can see your face. And I can tell, just as I would do with someone who is close to me and is sitting in front of me, what it is that you are thinking and feeling whether you say it or not. I understand your last letter. I do not know, because you are not telling me, if there is anything I can do or say to help you make decisions. If there is, you must make it plain to me. I know what I want for this new year, and it is more than the avoidance of disaster.

To my news, then, which is all joyful.

Erik collected Karin and the baby and drove them to my house for Christmas. It was wonderful. We none of us spoke much, even Erik who is more likely to chatter. We sat by the fire, and took turns to hold the baby. Erik and Karin cooked and the food was rich and full of flavour. In the afternoon, we took the baby, well wrapped up, and walked round the lake where we had floated Birgitt's ornaments away. This time

– only two nights, one day – was like one long, thick, sweet, hot drink, comforting and satisfying.

Karin had something to tell us, when she arrived, that would have worried me, at another time, but we none of us spoke of it, afterwards, and I found I could be detached. Was it good or bad, what she had to tell us? I could not say and would not let myself speculate. Her news was about Ben, the baby's father. She had not told me that he was still sending her e-mails and, as the pregnancy went on, she was answering them, but without telling him about the baby. She had told me that when she realised there could be problems for her or the baby, she began to think she was wrong to keep Ben from knowing about his daughter. When she was recovering in hospital, after the birth, she felt less sure. Then her friend found the book of poems you mentioned and one of these is about the father. About the father bringing the mother and baby home from hospital. It is addressed, by the mother, to the baby. The first line is: 'I want you to know'. It was this poem that convinced her and she sent Ben an e-mail. She was looking for nothing from him, she told him, but she now felt it was not her right to keep Birgitt and Ben ignorant of each other. She, Karin, could not say whether Ben would choose to know Birgitt now, or whether she, Birgitt, would choose to know him, when she was old enough to know her own mind. All Karin could be certain of was that until that day, she would not give up responsibility for Birgitt. She might not even be prepared to share that responsibility. All she was telling Ben, she said (to him and to us) was that this baby had been born out of her egg, his sperm.

He had replied, not with any complaints or even any expressions of joy, but with a flight time. He was going to arrive in

Copenhagen on the morning of 27th December. Karin told him she would meet him at the airport. Her idea was to take the baby. There would be no celebration of the first meeting of father and child, just a woman holding an infant in a crowded public space. Also, she would be able to judge, she thought, what her next steps should be – whether to invite him to the flat, for instance – once she had managed that first meeting, so it was important to arrange it so that all options of where he might stay or go next remained open. We, Erik and I, listened to her explaining all this and we said: 'Your choice, your decisions.' Then we all sat on the sofa and watched the flames in the stove and the light catching on the white, silver and gold-painted wooden globes I had hung from the ceiling.

Of course, when the time came for Erik to take Karin and Birgitt back to Copenhagen, on 26th December, I was full of worry. I said, should I come with you? No, she said. So I waited for all of the next day for word from her and on the following day, she phoned. She asked if she and Ben could come and stay with me, for two nights. Yes, I said, of course, and I asked no questions. I wonder if it is easier for families who have the habit of talking. If I had always used words to let my children know what I was thinking and feeling, would that have been a better way of bringing them up and loving them and going on supporting them now they are old enough to support themselves. I do not have that habit and at the least it means I did not say anything that was the wrong thing to say at the time.

When they arrived, I could see at once it might be possible to say the wrong thing. Both of them looked as if they were holding their breath. Ben is taller and bulkier than Karin and sort of tightly made – there must be a word, tell me what it is.

He is dark and serious. I had expected someone much looser, perhaps because – I can admit this to you – I was still rather shocked at the way he and Karin had behaved, when Birgitt was conceived, and, unfairly, I'm sure, I blamed him. But he is sober and hesitant, which I also did not expect, because I thought, from the story of what happened when Karin was alone in a crowd and being bothered by strangers, he would be confident and forceful.

When I opened the door, he was holding the baby and this made me hope that everything was going to be all right.

'We had to get out of Copenhagen,' Karin said, as she kissed me. 'Too many people.'

They stayed for three days and for the first two I did not see them very much. They went for walks and to places in the car, and they slept. Karin had one room, Ben another, but when the baby cried in the night I heard two sets of footsteps going to and fro with her. When they were not out or asleep, we sat and looked at the baby and talked about the most ordinary things: Ben's job and Karin's job; the book I am writing; Silkeborg; the town in Australia where Ben grew up. We spoke, of course, in English and I thought of your delight at the accents on the trains you travelled in. I find the English Ben spoke much more solid, in his mouth, than the English voices I usually hear in the museum.

As the days passed, I found out two things. Firstly, Ben is not so serious. He is diffident but in normal times he smiles a lot, makes jokes, behaves like someone who believes life is fun. I like that. Secondly, they were, slowly, letting go of the breath they were holding and, as they passed the baby between them, they were building trust in each other.

On the last night, Karin said:

'Ben has three sisters, all older than he is. His mother has eight grandchildren already.'

'Not one of them as cute as Birgitt,' Ben said.

Karin touched his hand. 'Obviously not, but my father talked about whether we should be worried your mother might need Birgitt to make her life complete, and I was just telling him it isn't so.'

'It was an honourable thought,' said Ben. 'Thank you for thinking it.'

Later, I said to Karin: 'I think it is time you went back to Copenhagen.'

'Tomorrow,' she said.

So they went and yesterday she phoned to tell me Ben has gone back to Australia. Before Karin goes back to work, she will visit him. Then he will visit her. They have given themselves a year to decide if they want to live on the same continent, in the same town, in the same apartment. Then, if the answer is yes, they will look at jobs available for him and for her and decide which continent, which town that will be. I hope the answer is yes. I hope the continent is Europe and the town is Copenhagen. But I do not mind. I am like a man standing on a shore watching people he loves rowing a boat. As long as they are safe in the boat, nothing else is so important.

I am alone in the house now, when I am not in my office making notes for the book. Write soon for I have no one else to talk to.

Love,
Anders

Inverness
12th January

My Dear Anders,

Here it is, the bear. Only a little bear, as you will see, so fitting easily inside this envelope. I am posting this in Inverness, before I leave for home. I am waiting until I reach home, and my own computer, to see if you have written to me again. Something to look forward to. Although going home is also something to look forward to. I have enjoyed myself with Mary and Vassily, but there are things I will not miss when I am back at the farm. It is a little cramped, in a caravan, even a big, two-bedroomed mobile-home type of caravan such as Mary and Vassily have. It feels like an insubstantial place to lie down and sleep. Also, it is hard to know what they are hoping I will do – cooking? cleaning? – and what they are hoping I will not interfere with – cooking? cleaning? They have been most welcoming and took me into Inverness to see the town and round the lochs and the mountains to see the scenery, but I felt I was an interruption. They have much to do: building the house, obviously, and keeping the caravan clean, but also building up the life they have chosen to lead. I sense that this is harder, more emotionally demanding than they thought it would be when they left the farm. They were so merry and excited, then. Now they are more thoughtful and sombre. But still happy. Still contented, one with the other.

I will write again when I am home, and respond to whatever you have told me in the letter I am expecting to find.

Much love,

Tina

Silkeborg
18th January

Dear Tina,

The bear – does he have a name? – is sitting on my desk, watching me as I write. He has his back to the window, of course, because I am facing it. I will give him to Birgitt when next I see her but I am not in a hurry to pass him on. It will be months before she will be able to look at him and recognise him and I can look at him and recognise him now. So I am keeping hold of him, to add to my collection of a feather, a square of cloth and the letters. I like the way you have made his mouth turn up in a smile. I can imagine you were smiling as you did this piece of sewing. I am smiling, looking at Mr Bear's smile and picturing your hands holding him as mine are holding him now.

I think I will give Mr Bear a name. I wanted to name him after the man who was part of the team sent to dig the Tollund Man out of the peat and transport him to Copenhagen, under the direction of Professor Glob. This man did not reach Copenhagen but died of a heart attack whilst the excavation was taking place. I have always thought how sad it was to die lifting such a find as the Tollund Man out of the earth never having the chances we have to learn more about this body, so well preserved. Never to have left the bog alive, and yet not to have his body preserved as the Tollund Man's was. Though his body is long gone, I thought that giving his name to this little bear would be giving him the chance to take part in the later stages of the story which he never lived through. However, I have not been able, sitting here at home, to find out what this man's name was, so I believe I will call the bear Peter after Professor Glob.

Professor Glob is, after all, responsible for introducing us to each other, so to say. If you had already named him, you must tell me.

Thinking of names has made me remember seminars I have taken part in, with archaeologists, curators and conservators, which were arranged by the marketing people responsible for making visible and understandable to people who are not archaeologists, curators and conservators, what it is we work with so diligently. The seminars were intended to find more ways to make this happen – the visibility and the understandability (is that a word?) – and one of the topics the marketing people wanted us to discuss was giving names to the bog people. Calling the Tollund Man Knut, for example; the Elling woman Eva. I argued strongly against this. The figures, which have been preserved through a combination of circumstances, are people unknown to us. It would be an empty pretence to give them names from which, before long, we would create characters. They were known to those they lived among and to those who killed them. They are known to us only as men and women so perfectly preserved they might almost, but not quite, be asleep. To give them names, said the marketing people, would make them seem more human. But, I said (and not only me, fortunately) to give them names would make them *only* human, rob them of their mystery.

The knitted bear has made me remember all this and now I am wondering about my idea of giving a man's name to an object made of wool. But I think in using his name I am paying homage to Professor Glob. If we gave the Tollund Man a name that was not his we would be insisting on knowing him as if he was a man like us.

Tell me what you think.

Thank you for the bear. I did not remember to say that at first.

Love,
Anders

Silkeborg
6th February

Dear Tina,

You must forgive me for writing before you have answered my last letter, but I have become impatient. Is that word too harsh? I mean to say I am impatient for your reply and it has not come, and I am fearful that this is because I have upset you in some way, or because something has occurred to prevent you from writing to me, and then, of course, I begin to imagine what that might be. I do not think of myself as someone with a good imagination, but in the matter of thinking of disasters that might happen, my imagination is too good. Last night I could not sleep and I went downstairs and sat facing the window in the dark, with the moonlight picking out the shapes of my few ornaments and giving me just enough light to see that, however sad I might be feeling, Peter the bear is still smiling. This made me hopeful that you are also still smiling and have some reason for your silence that is a joyful reason, which you will explain to me when you have time. I resolved I would write to you again without waiting longer, just to tell you that I am missing hearing from you. You have made it possible for me to talk of things I have never spoken of before, and to understand what has been hidden. I am peaceful, now, as I was not before; happier. I wanted you to know.

Love,
Anders

Dear Anders,

I wish I could stitch a smile onto my face to match the smile on the bear, but I cannot. Everything has changed. No. Nothing has changed. It is just that I have all at once discovered that I was wrong in the way I understood everything to be. I have your letter about Karin and your letter about the bear. I think maybe we should stop there. With you, happy. With me, having shared your happiness. I do not want to burden you with my unhappiness.

Tina

Dear Tina,

I do not understand. How can we stop? You must know how important it has been to me, talking to you. You have brought me from misery to happiness. Without ever seeing your face, touching your hand, sharing a meal. I cannot believe you would deny me the chance to do the same for you. You must tell me what has happened. Please.

I will not stop thinking about you and wondering what it is, until you write again. I will not stop writing to you, until you reply to me.

Love,

Anders

Bury St Edmunds
16th February

Dear Anders,

I am sorry. You are right. I owe you an explanation. I thought I would be unable to write this down, but now I remember that writing things down, to send to you, has been helpful to me. Perhaps telling you the story will be helpful again.

I came home from Inverness a day earlier than I had planned. I found Mary, Vassily and I had spent as much time together as we needed to, for the moment, in the circumstances. So I caught a train home and texted Andrew to come and pick me up when I arrived in the evening. This time I changed at Edinburgh as well as York and Peterborough and the daylight, while it lasted, was grey and foggy and the darkness was murky, all the lights we passed fuzzy with mist. I was beyond weariness by the time I reached Bury St Edmunds. Andrew was waiting for me past the ticket barrier and I was relieved to see him there, ready to take my case, to give me a hug. I had thought I would be pleased to be home but when we drove into the yard, I felt no pleasure at all. Just a dull sense of a tiring journey ended. I walked in out of the mist and there was Edward, sitting in his shirtsleeves with his collar and his hair ruffled up from taking off his overalls, with a pot of tea made, keeping it warm with a tea cosy I knitted years ago. In a diamond pattern. I was proud of myself for having knitted something so complicated, at the time, and whenever I have noticed it since – it is used every day but you know how it is with things you use every day; you only become aware of them once in a while – I have been pleased to know I made it, and it is handsome, and well made.

I felt warm, for a moment, noticing the nice tea cosy, knowing Edward had taken his overalls off and made the tea because he knew I would appreciate it. The tea would be too strong, and the overalls would be lying on the floor in the scullery waiting for me to pick them up and put them in the washing machine, but still. He had tried. I drank the tea and Edward told me everything that had occurred since I left (though not quite everything, but I will come to that). What he said was familiar to me. He talked as he always does, but I heard it more clearly because I listened with the recent memory of how Mary and Vassily had talked, to me and to each other. Edward told me everything that occurred which had annoyed him. A walker not in control of her dogs; a planning application for a solar farm which would mean construction traffic on the lanes; the failure of an agricultural machinery supplier to deliver a part within the promised twenty-four hours; no beef dripping in the fridge when he fancied a slice of toast; a favourite pair of socks which he had looked for all over the place and failed to find. If anything good had happened in my absence, he did not think to mention it.

If I had not been so tired, I would have gone at once to find the beef dripping and the socks. I knew pretty well where both of them would be. I realise, of course, that it is because I have always gone at once to find the things Edward wants, that he can never find them. He has no capacity for searching; why should he have, when he has only to call my name and whatever it is will be found. But that night I was too tired and these things he had lost – he was struggling to remember what else it was he had looked for and could not find, for there was definitely something else – were not needed at that moment, so I went to bed.

I expected the bedroom to be a trampled mess of discarded clothes and dirty sheets. But it was as clean and tidy as I had left it, and this, like the tea and the tea cosy and the discarded overalls, made me feel I should appreciate Edward's little kindnesses, which do not come naturally to him and therefore represent a deliberate effort. So tidy was the bedroom, I wondered briefly if he had slept in another room, to leave it as he knew I would like to find it, but I fell asleep before I had half completed this thought.

When I woke up in the morning, Edward was already gone. I lay looking around the bedroom and thought: Edward must have asked Sarah to come in and make the bed. But the sheets were the ones I had put on it before I left. Another room, then, I said to myself. I would look after breakfast, because it would be my job to restore it to order.

You will be ahead of me by now. Wondering why I am wasting so much paper on tea cosies and clean sheets. Did I know, while I was brushing my teeth, pulling on my jumper, combing my hair? I could not say. I was still safe in the before; I may have known there would be an after but it was not yet.

I went down to the kitchen. Tam and Andrew were there, as well as Edward. They had the tang of fresh air on them, the sharpness of wind still on their clothes and in their hair. Andrew stood up to pour me a cup of coffee from the pot on the stove and I said, to Edward, as I sat down, idly, idly as if this were a question just brushing the edge of my mind, to be dealt with before matters of more substance were discussed:

'Where have you been sleeping, while I've been away?'

'What?' said Edward, as if he hadn't heard me. But he had heard me and, for the first time, I heard myself; understood the question I had been asking myself since I went to bed the night before. I looked up and round at the three faces watching me and all that I thought I knew and understood about my life dropped away and left me with no clue who this person was, who had lived in this house for all these years. Given birth to these children. Been a wife to this man.

I can hardly bear to keep writing but I will stick to the story. If I get that down, it may be easier to say what is important. To explain how I feel.

Tam stood up and walked out of the kitchen. Andrew stayed. Edward said:

'I don't know what you're implying.'

'I was asking,' I said, 'if you had slept in one of the spare rooms.'

I looked square into his face. He has a high colour from the life he has led. His eyes are blue and surrounded by thousands of lines. The lines are threads of white against the bronze of his cheeks, for he is a man ready to smile or ready to frown and whenever he does either, his face creases up, and the lines are in the folds of skin protected from the weather. It was what I noticed: the depth of colour on his face and the lines standing out in the blankness of his expression. What he said next mattered. I was certain he had not slept in another room in the house, without going to check. Or, if he had, it was not alone. I could see it in his face, in Andrew's face, in Tam's quick retreat. Had he lied to me, then, I cannot say what I would have done. I might have struck him, though I have never hit anyone in my life and would probably not have been capable of it. I might have thrown something, broken something, vomited on the floor. If he had lied I would have lost all the dignity I was holding on to until I had time to understand what was happening to me.

But he did not lie. He turned his head and asked Andrew to go. Then he told me the truth. The facts, that is. I understood those. I have more difficulty understanding everything else he said, about how he felt, what he thought, and I do not know how much of it to believe.

The facts. He has been in a relationship with another woman for over a year. He has visited her house on the afternoons when I thought he was playing golf, on some of the evenings when I thought he was at meetings, in the pub, attending formal dinners. He has spent less time at the market, the agricultural merchants', neighbouring farms than he told me. More with her. On the rare occasions when I have been away overnight, or the slightly more frequent occasions when he has had an excuse to stay away – conferences, golfing trips – he has spent the night at her house. I have never noticed. I have never had one moment's suspicion.

At first, I was furious. I do not feel angry, truly angry, very often. I do not readily recognise insult, or believe I have the right to resent it at the pitch that would make anger an appropriate response. When Edward finished telling me the story, I was so angry I could not speak. And what was causing this was not the betrayal – which is what matters and I will come to that – but the detail. The woman he has been having an affair with (why do we use such a word to describe it? What does 'affair' mean? It sounds light and airy and I told myself not to use it, but there it is, slid on to the screen) is Daphne Trigg. Daphne Trigg. A woman I despise. Whose opinions and attitudes are banal, ill informed and prejudiced. Whose interests are narrow, trivial and entirely self-centred. I might – though I probably wouldn't – have been able to swallow the enormity of my husband being attracted to a woman so offensively ordinary and dull, if she had been physically much more appealing than me. I have no very high opinion of my own appearance and I am ready to admit that Daphne may be, or have been, prettier than I am, or have ever been, but she is not in a different league. Both of us can only claim a place in the category of women who are neither ugly nor beautiful. She is younger, by six or seven years, but overweight and with no idea at all of how a woman of her age and figure ought to dress. I may be careless in what I wear, but I am not ridiculous.

Not only (I feel as if I am starting to rant. Forgive me. This is how I felt at the time and the bile is rising in my throat as I think of it again) has Edward chosen to betray me with someone I cannot recognise as a more appealing companion in any way – emotional, conversational or physical – he has also chosen to do it within our social, even familial, circle. Although I would have said we did not know them well, Daphne and her husband had been known to us for years, used to go to the same events we went to. She knows other women I know well and amongst whom I count several as friends. I may not be the only one out of this whole group who knew nothing of what was going on, but those who knew, I feel sure, are in the majority. For the last few months she had

become part of the family by being part of the farm. I have a
right to be furious.

Later, when I had walked out of the kitchen, leaving Edward
in mid-self-exculpatory sentence, and hidden myself in the
chicken shed in order to think, I began to realise how much
more important than the choice of Daphne Trigg was the
betrayal itself. I had been, as you know, puzzling over
the matter of how my life had turned out and why, but I
thought at least I understood what that life was. The weft and
the warp of it. The firm ground and the boggy. I thought I
knew where it was roughly darned and where neatly patched
but despite all the flaws in the fabric, I believed in the essential wholeness of it.

I understood there was no passion between Edward and
me. That there were topics that interested me and not him;
topics that interested him and not me. I understood that I had
become a farmer's wife and, whether I would have chosen it
or not, I did the job as well as I was able. I understood that
I did this through loyalty to Edward, who had, through all
the years, provided me with companionship and comforts. I
owed him this loyalty because, for all the lack of passion and
the topics avoided, he was a good man. I thought the choice I
had made was the wrong one for me, but as long as it worked
for him I had to make it work for us both, because he was a
good man. So I thought; loyal to me, I would have said. But I
was wrong. Being wrong in this fundamental way, how could
I now make sense of the life we had led together? All these
years, in a house I did not choose, what was the point of it?
How much of a fool had I been?

I sat on the filthy straw in the chicken shed for so long, so quiet, so still, that a couple of birds came up and began pecking at my boots to see if by chance any titbit suitable for a chicken might have become wedged in the tread. A hen set up a racket to let the world know she had laid an egg and another rushed up to give her a peck as she came out of the nesting box. If I could have fitted in the nesting box, I think I would have crawled into it, to be safe from the curiosity and malice of the hens I live among.

I have difficulty avoiding Edward. He keeps looking for me, trying to explain himself, to excuse himself, to reassure me. It is too hard to think, so I have decided to leave, at least until I have understood better what all this means. I feel I can count on nothing. I have to look at everything I have done and thought afresh, with this new knowledge. Writing to you is one of the things I need to think about. I must ask you to be patient with me. Not to answer this letter. I know whatever you say will be thoughtful and kind and I cannot bear it. Please wait until I can bring myself round into a position where I can be sure my feet are planted squarely on firmer ground.

Tina

Silkeborg
27th February

Dear Tina,

I have waited for your next letter, as you asked me to do, but I am finding it hard to fill the hours. You must know how important it has been to me, talking to you. What must I do now? Receive visits from my family; make visits to my family;

go to work. But when I am doing none of these things? In the hours and hours I would want to spend thinking about what you said to me last, what I will say to you next? When I should be noticing things, to tell you of them, when I should be noticing things because you have told me to notice them. It is not just the hours I cannot fill. There is a part of me that feels empty when I do not hear from you.

I have passed some time reading again all the letters I have received from you. At the beginning – do you remember? – you told me you and Bella were always planning to visit the Tollund Man. When things were bad for her because of the battle with her ex-husband over the child, you said one of you would suggest now was the moment. The other would say no, it was not. I am sure if Bella was still alive, she would be telling you to come, and there is no reason why you should not. You have saved up this trip, so you seem to say, for the right moment. This is the right moment. Visit Silkeborg. The museum is open every day. Transport is easy. The sky, the weather patterns, the landscape may be the same in Bury St Edmunds as it is in Silkeborg. But from here, the view will be different.

I will wait for you. I would come to you, if you wished it, but I think we should meet for the first time here. Under the same roof as the Tollund Man.

If you do not answer this I will not know if you have received it, and chosen not to answer it, or if it has not reached you, wherever you are. I say this, of course, to make it harder for you not to reply.

I will say nothing about what you told me in your last letter, because I do not feel I have the right to do so unless you ask what my opinion is. What my feelings are. What I can say is that I think of you every day and I feel pain on your behalf.

Love,

Anders

Bella's Flat
Bury St Edmunds
5th March

Dear Anders,

You made it hard for me not to answer, that is true. It is also true that I wanted to write to you, but while this is true, it is not necessarily right. I will come to this.

I am living in Bella's old flat in town. It belongs to Alicia, now, and she put it up for sale after Bella died, but she has not tried to sell it. She has ignored the estate agent's requests to tidy it up, redecorate, rearrange, and she has refused the couple of offers she has had. Meanwhile, she has come back several times to stay in it – her home is still in Italy. Because she has not cleared the flat of all Bella's things, it still feels like her place, somewhere she may yet be, only in another room. It still smells as it did when Bella was alive. I think this is why Alicia is trying not to part with it. Each time she came over I visited her here, and each time it has felt like a refuge. I thought it was Alicia's refuge, but now it is mine.

Although there is clutter in the flat, as there is at home, it is clutter that has the possibility of movement within it. It is made of what might be, at any moment, picked up and used. Piles of books to be read; articles cut from magazines and not yet filed or thrown out; slippers waiting for the moment when the door is locked for the night and a descent into comfort and idleness can begin. Not like the hardened crust of useless ornament that fills the farmhouse. When I realised I could no longer stay there, I arranged with Alicia that I could come here. I shut the door behind me, took Bella's purple embroidered jacket out of the wardrobe and cried and cried into it. Until I could almost hear her voice telling me to stop. To take control.

I have been here for a week now and I still feel, when I come back into the flat, the same shock of Bella's absence and the opposite sense of being warm and safe. I have tidied up, but only to the extent of making orderly piles, throwing out the rubbish, scrubbing the kitchen surfaces and replacing the pans I could not bring back to a standard I would accept for preparing food. I hope I have reached a balance between keeping it as Alicia still needs it to be – full of Bella – and making it comfortable to live in.

Now I have come to the end of the things that are easy to write about. I have been turning over all the other topics I could fill the pages with – lists of the scarves Bella owned, anecdotes about the places I have found stray earrings, an analysis of her musical tastes as demonstrated by her CD collection. But really, why would you care to read any of this? When I know you are waiting for me to tell you the state of my emotions, the state of my marriage. So much harder to describe.

Let me tell you, first, what I now know. I know who knew when I did not.

Andrew. He says he worked it out only when Daphne began to come into the office every day, seeing them together so often. I might have done too, if I had seen them together, but they were more careful with me; I rarely did see them together. Even if I had, my blindness was so complete it would have taken more than a shared glance to illuminate it. Knowing has been hard for Andrew, I see now. He is uncertain and unhappy but we have not found a way to talk about it.

Tam. I think he has known from the start. He is treating the business as a major inconvenience Edward and I are inflicting on him. He wants nothing to do with it and he is not interested in who is to blame. We are both equally at fault for the crime he perceives we have committed – upsetting the smooth running of the farm and undermining his comfort.

Sarah. I don't know how long she has known and I am not going to find out because I feel the smirk behind her sympathy like a pin left behind in the seam of a jumper I have just finished sewing up.

Various friends. I know they know because they have called to offer shoulders to cry on, and they must have been aware of the relationship to have picked up so quickly that it had been exposed. I do not cry on shoulders. It has never been something I did or wanted to do. (Until now. I am crying on yours, my dear Anders. How can I bear it?)

Mary did not know. This is a huge relief; if she had done, I must believe she would have said something. She tells me she was uneasy, but not about Daphne.

I know now that Edward has been giving Daphne, or allowing Daphne to take, money. I know this because she made sure I did. Edward had not mentioned it and, in truth, I could not care less. But Daphne obviously wanted me to know. She came out of the office when I went back to the farm to fetch a few clothes and spoke to me in the yard. I expected the sight of her to make me furious, all over again, but as soon as she tottered up in her high-heeled shoes and began to patronise me, I felt sorry for her. I realised she is as much a victim in all this as I am. She told me she was sorry and she had not wanted me to find out but maybe it is all for the best, because, of course, it has been hard on Edward. He is such a kind man he could not bear the thought of hurting me, and this was why he had kept it secret. It had been harder still for her, though, not being able to live openly with the man she loved. He had made sure she did not suffer financially because of his soft-heartedness towards me. She hoped there would be no hard feelings between us.

I wondered, listening to all this, whether she believes Edward wants to replace me with her, or whether she is trying to convince herself he does. He does not, I could have told her, but didn't. She is deluding herself, as she will soon find out. I may not have been as much fun to be with as she is, but I have always been much more useful. I cannot imagine that Daphne would cook and clean, wash and iron, work on the farm, keep the cupboards stocked with everything anyone opening the cupboard would expect to be there, know where anything that might be needed could be found, mend whatever needed mending, make appointments for the doctor, the dentist, the hairdresser, the chiropodist, the vet, and remember to remind everyone when these were. If Edward wants Daphne to do all this, and more, he would have to ask her to do it. And even if she agrees, she would not do it without complaint. And even if she agrees, and carries out whatever she has agreed to do, it would not be to a satisfactory standard. I have seen her at work in the office, and she would not suit Edward in the role of wife rather than lover. He knows that. He does not want me to leave him, which is something else I know, now the first storm is over, but Daphne does not. So as I stood there in the yard, hand on the car door, feet in a smear of slurry, listening to her voice, raised to compete with the wind, telling me how perfectly it had all worked out, I pitied her. And, although it is not easy being me at this moment, at least I can be grateful I am not Daphne Trigg.

The things I still don't know are: why did Edward do it; what happens next; what am I in all this?

Edward has given me many explanations for being unfaithful. They vary with his mood. When he is feeling aggrieved because I do not respond, he tells me it is all my fault. I am cold, uncaring. I have never been wholeheartedly enthusiastic about his enthusiasms. This is true. When he is in despair at the idea I might abandon him, he says it is all his fault; he has appetites and has been unable to control them. This may be true. When he is both aggrieved and in despair, he says it is all Daphne's fault. She seduced him. I do not think this is true.

What happens next? I do not know what Edward thinks will happen next. I know he does not want me to go, but he has also said nothing that would lead me to think he is prepared to end the relationship with Daphne to make me stay. I think he is waiting; he does not know what I am thinking about what happens next. Now I am going to come to the part that is hard.

When I first found out I reacted with outrage. I felt like an innocent woman, grossly deceived by those she had trusted, those she had served. But once I calmed down, I began to challenge my own innocence. Because of you. We have never met; how can a correspondence with you be compared to a recurring act of physical infidelity? I can imagine you exclaiming to yourself. Let me explain. The least important part of what Edward has done, as far as I am concerned, is the sex. So what? If he had strayed in this way a dozen times, with casual strangers, I might have been disappointed, thought him weak, but it would not have made so much difference to our life as a couple. I have often wondered, in fact, if this had happened, and supposed, on balance, it probably had; now I am reasonably certain it must have done. What is so overwhelming about the relationship with Daphne Trigg, though, is that it is a relationship sustained over time and therefore has an emotional dimension. He turned away from me as a person, not simply as a sexual partner. Do you begin to see? I am doing exactly that. I am reaching out to you as a partner in my emotions and I have kept this secret from my husband because we, you and I, have approached a level of intimacy in this context that would make him feel excluded and diminished. At least, if I imagine our positions were reversed and I uncovered such a correspondence as you and I have been having between Edward and another woman, it would make me feel excluded and diminished, and I have to assume it would be the same for him.

I said earlier that Mary was uneasy, although she knew nothing about her father's infidelity. I was the one making her uneasy. Because I had shared our correspondence with her, she had begun to understand the distance separating Edward and me. She had seen the possibility our marriage would break down, not because of anything he had said or done, but because of what I was saying and doing.

I cannot tell Edward I am leaving and walk out with my head held high. I have to think carefully about where both of us have ended up. It is possible that the timing of his affair, soon after I started writing to you, is not a coincidence; that

ANNE YOUNGSON

I may have withdrawn further from him because I was more interested in what we were saying to each other than in what Edward was saying to me. More interested in you than in him. I have to make an effort to see if there is a route back to where we started from. I owe it to him because I am not innocent. Do you understand? There. I have asked you a question. You have the right to reply to it. Whatever reply you send, I will read.

No matter what happens next, you must know this correspondence has been important to me; life-enhancing, liberating. I do not know if I have expressed to you how much it has meant to me; I have been, I think, less generous and more reserved than you have been. Now I feel I must tell you: it has filled all the crevices in my heart and mind. But it has moved me away from the place I stepped into when I married Edward more than forty years ago, and that is not right.

Tina

Silkeborg
8th March

Dearest Tina,

I do understand. But I do not agree. This may be a long letter. I know you will read it to the end. I have put together my ideas as best I can and hope that this will be enough.

Let me say a few words first about grief. This is something I understand. When you describe how it is to be in your friend Bella's flat, it reminds me of an office Birgitt rented in Aarhus. Did I even mention this? I believe not. She was a designer by training and when we were first married she worked for

184

an agency designing advertisements and posters and leaflets, but it did not suit her to be employed, so she began to do freelance design jobs, when she was well enough. At first she worked at the house, but she wanted to keep this part of her life separate from her home and her family, so we rented an office in Aarhus. When she had a commission, she would go by train in the morning and come home in the evening. They were bad days for me. I would wait at the station and until the very moment when I saw her coming towards me, I would be certain I would never see her again. I hated that her office was in Aarhus – it is too far off for me to be able to reach it quickly and also, it is by the sea. I imagined she would one day, leaving her office, turn away from the station and go instead to the shore, to the harbour, and find a way to drift off in search of whatever she had lost as a child. But she never did. I think I misunderstood how her work fitted into her life. She was always trying to keep her balance and later I thought that this office was at one end of the see-saw (I have had to look this word up; I like it), and was the dull, detailed weight against the pull of the ocean and freedom from depression at the other end. The children and I were in the middle, so she would never have gone from the office to the sea without passing me on the way.

After she died, I did not go to the office for some weeks. I almost forgot about it but then I noticed I was still paying rent and I drove over to Aarhus to empty it. I had not been there for years, and it was completely unfamiliar, when I opened the door, yet it was as if Birgitt had that moment just left. Or rather, as if she was still there but hiding from me. Although the room was small, it was arranged in such a way that who-ever was in it could be tucked away behind a chair, under the desk, between the blind and the window. By the time she died, all Birgitt's work was done on a computer; she designed websites, mostly, and did not need the drawing boards and cupboards full of paper and card and pencils and paints she had used when she first started. In their place, she had brought in cushions and blankets and created nests. I have never been into a room so full and so empty. I could not leave, but it was too hard to move. As I stood there in the doorway a young man came up the stairs with a cup of coffee, going to his own office on a higher floor. He rescued me. He sent me to buy a cup of coffee for myself and when I came back, he had drawn up the blinds and folded the blankets and picked up the cushions so it looked like a room full of nothing but furniture. He stayed with me all morning, and other people from the building came to help, bringing boxes to pack away the files and bags to put rubbish in. There were objects, too. I had never seen any of them before but if someone had laid them out on a table in the street I was walking along, I would have been able to say, as I passed, 'my wife collected these together'. They had nothing to do with me and nothing to do with each other and I put them in a box and left them with the kind tenants of the other offices, to throw away or give away or keep as they wished. As we did at last with the objects she left in the house (with some help from you).

I did not mean to talk about this at such length: only to describe my own feelings about a room like Bella's flat, both full of a person who has gone and yet empty. But it has made me think, as I am writing, of other points I will make, further on.

You say you cannot believe yourself to be innocent because of the letters you have written to me and received from me.

My first thought was: this is not so. What if, I thought, I was a young man of twenty-four, or an old man of eighty-four, as I might well have been. Then no one would find any fault in the letters we have exchanged. You would have been guilty of nothing except kindness, to a boy with everything to learn or to an old man with nothing to fill his days. But as I tried to develop this thought into an argument I could put to you, to stop you from rejecting our friendship, I saw it was weak. Our letters have meant so much to us because we have both arrived at the same point in our lives. More behind us than ahead of us. Paths chosen that define us. Enough time left to change. So I will say at once – these letters have made a connection between us that puts us in a position of being the closest of friends. Even though we have never met. I am more interested in your opinion than I am in the opinions of people I meet every day. I like you more than the people I meet every day. If we were to meet, I believe the feelings I have for you could go beyond liking to love. I will rewrite that sentence. When we do meet, I believe the feelings I have for you will go beyond liking to love. Despite what I have just written, I am still not agreeing with you that you are in some way guilty. Guilt is a matter of circumstances. Circumstances are never straightforward. Let me tell you a story from my childhood.

When I was sixteen years old and still living with my parents in Aarhus, I was walking through the park one evening when it was growing dark. There was no one about. A child ran out of some bushes beside where I was walking, a young child, maybe three or four years old. When she saw me, she ran up to me, crying because she had lost her mother. I looked around. No one. I took hold of the child's hand and walked round the bushes and then, as I could still see no one and the child was so upset, I set off to walk to my home with her. I could not think of anything else to do. I have a sister, younger than me, and I acted as if this child was my sister. I left the park and went three or four hundred metres along the pavement when the child's mother rushed up behind me, screaming the girl's name, snatching her hand from mine. It seemed she had been only a little distance away at the time the little girl came out of the bushes. She was just outside the park, strapping her baby into the car, and while she was distracted, the girl had run away, back into the park, to carry on the hiding game they had been playing. When she realised the child had gone, the mother thought first of the traffic and the busy streets and ran up and down the pavements, calling out to passers-by to help her look for her daughter. So as well as the mother, there were other people, men and women, crowded round me. I thought (I was only sixteen and not very mature) they would congratulate me for having found the one who was lost. But of course they only saw a youth holding the hand of a child and walking that child away from her mother. One of the crowd declared himself to be a policeman and took my name and address, then put me into his car and drove me home, to confirm my story. He told my mother what had happened, condemning what I had done. I should never have led the child away from the park. I should have stayed where I was and shouted for help, or walked to the nearest gate and stopped the first person passing, asked them to contact the police. I was technically, the policeman said, guilty of abduction.

While he was in the house, my mother agreed with what he said but when he had gone, she told me 'guilty' was the wrong word. It implies knowing what is right and choosing the opposite path. She said I had – now I am sure there is a perfect English word for it which you will tell me but I can only guess – stumbled. I had done a wrong thing but believed it to be right. (I realise at this point in the story you must think there are always children being lost in Denmark because I have also told you the story of Birgitt as a child, but the two events do not connect themselves in my mind. The child I found was playing at being lost.)

When I think of what happened that evening, I can see that, if I was guilty, if I did stumble, it was because the circumstances had made it inevitable. If the mother had been more careful to keep the child close to her; if the child had been taught not to run away even in fun; if I had not been brought up to believe it was my responsibility to take care of my sister, then this would not have happened.

I am sure you are so far ahead of me. Understand just what I am trying to say, with this little story from so long ago. The mother was a good mother, the child was a good child (we met, later, when everything was calm, and I know this) and I was a good boy. Despite this, what might have been a tragedy for all of us or some of us nearly happened.

Edward, you have told me, although before you knew the truth, is a good man. You are an honest woman. It is the circumstance of your marriage to each other that has created the situation where he has, quite definitely, betrayed you and you have stumbled (I will use that word again) into behaving in a way you, as an honest woman, do not feel you should behave towards the man you married. In the story I have told you, the responsibility for the events was mainly the mother's. She admitted this after it was all over. Whose is the responsibility for the events in your story, would you say? You are both guilty of wanting more than you were getting from your marriage to each other. Perhaps you should have tried to find more, but that would have required one of you or both of you to sacrifice something and you have already told me that the life you have led as a result of the decision to marry was a sacrifice.

Your parents, his parents, you, Edward were all involved in putting together this marriage. If it is failing, who can say where the blame for that lies – with those who conspired to make it happen in the first place, or with whoever took the first step that risked bringing it to an end? And I am not sure that is you. We may have been writing to each other for longer than Edward has been sleeping with Daphne Trigg, but Edward knew he was acting outside the rules, from the start. You were only looking for some way to understand who you had become. It is lucky – for once, the English word seems weak to me – lucky that through this need for understanding we found each other. You cannot believe that there is an equal fault in what you are doing, writing to me, and what Edward is doing. So now, I will be practical. Use the approach I would take to making decisions at work. What are the options? What are the implications of each of the options? Let me list them.

1. No Change. You and Edward stay living together at the farm. He continues to see Daphne Trigg and our friendship continues to develop. The only change is that now, you both know the truth.

When you went to the chicken hut on the day you found out, this would have appeared to be impossible, not to be thought about. But it is my experience that compromise is the easiest option for everyone to agree to. 'All right,' the conversation goes, 'it might not be the perfect solution, does not address the root of the problem, but, after all, it is a workable alternative without any major negative implications.' So meetings that start with a certainty that whatever else happens, things have to change, end with a decision to shift just a little to one side or the other but otherwise leave everything just as it was.

You will understand why this is a bad idea, but I will just remind you: you would surely lose your self-respect; you would know that you could not trust to the future, for change might still be unavoidable; nothing would change for the better. On the other hand, it would preserve your marriage, which is something I do not want to appear to suggest is not important.

Although I know you have described yourself as always on the side of balance, which means compromise, I cannot believe you are the sort of person who would agree to this option.

2. Restoration. You and Edward stay living together at the farm. He ends his relationship with Daphne Trigg. You stop your correspondence with me.

This path is the one an optimist would take. Someone with a belief that, with a little effort and good will, what has not worked in the past can be made to work in the future. It is the option that would seem to have no drawbacks. It is like restoring a corrupted computer to an earlier setting, when everything was operating normally. It assumes that the virus can be eliminated. This choice would be a catastrophe for me, but I want the best outcome for you, and if this is what you hope for, I would like it to be the one that you and Edward choose. I will only say, before you do: no chance of finding the raspberries left unpicked. No new fronds unfurling.

3. Retribution. You stay at the farmhouse and Edward leaves, goes to live with Daphne Trigg but continues (it is his job) to run the farm.

When I first thought about the options I overlooked this one. It would be the choice of someone who likes the role of martyr, likes to punish, even if the pain of the punishment is shared. I cannot imagine you as this person.

4. Revolution. You leave.

Where you go, what life you create for yourself, these are decisions that, having made the first decision, you would need to come to in time. The options are too many to list. Too many raspberries to count. You would have to decide just two things at the beginning – where to go at first and how much time you needed to make the next choice. (Which could, of course, include a version of any of the above.)

It takes courage to go down this path. I am hopeful you have courage. We are different, I realise, in the way we respond to bad news. You had the courage to be angry, where I think I would have fallen into sorrow, melancholy. In a way, Birgitt was only pretending to be married to me, as Edward has pretended faithfulness to you. Our lives together were full of tenderness, but sad. The children were impatient with her, sometimes, even angry, but I was only ever able to respond to her with sympathy and care. Maybe I allowed her to indulge herself. She might have been better able to cope if I had been more forceful, insisted it was possible. I like it that you are angry. You can be forceful with Edward, insist on an end to the relationship.

I cannot hide from you how much I hope, for your sake as well as mine, that you choose the revolutionary path.

I said I would refer back to Birgitt's empty office. It is the emptiness I wanted you to think about. If, as a result of a decision you make now, there will be absences of those now present in your life, which of those absences will leave the greatest emptiness in the room?

I will wait.

Love,

Anders

Scotland
20th March

My Dear Anders,

I have chosen. I think I was always going to make this choice. Or maybe not without you. I am somewhere unknown to me where I am unknown. I am in a cottage on the west coast of Scotland watching the weather arrive from across the Atlantic and change the appearance of the hills, rocks and sea as it passes. This is all I can see from the windows – hills, rocks and sea. I have been nowhere since I arrived, four days ago now. Tomorrow I will drive up and down the folds of empty land to reach a place where I can buy the few things I need for comfort – bread, milk, cheese and wine. I have enough books. I have enough firewood. I have passed through the anger and anguish and have found something like contentment. Sadness may be over the horizon but it has not yet blown in.

I had made no decisions when I read your last letter; I was not in a state of mind to make a decision. In fact, I had hardly grasped that it might be mine to make. It was in my mind, as I said in my last letter to you, that I was not innocent, and that I owed it to Edward to try and find a way through this that would hold our marriage together. I was waiting, I think, for him to declare what he was prepared to do, what promises he would make, what compromises he might suggest to allow us to go forward. Or go back, rather, to some version of the life we had led before. When I read the choices you suggested were open to me, I began to think about my marriage, for the first time, as something that was not fixed. If this were so, I thought, how might I alter it? I was still thinking in a detached way; as if the decisions were not mine to make; as if I had to wait for something else to happen which would make the next thing happen and so allow life to go on without a decision ever having been made.

Something did happen. Edward sent a message asking if he could arrange a time to meet with me. We needed to move forward, he said. This was a verbal message. I would recognise his handwriting if he wrote to me, from lists, instructions and reminders scribbled out and left on the table or pinned to a beam in the barn. I do not think I have ever received anything personal to me, though, that he has written. I might have cherished a note, even now, but he was not to know that. He did as he would always have done – asked Andrew to deliver a message to me. I sent a message back. A verbal message. (If I am being fair, which I am trying to be, I have written very little to Edward that is personal. An occasional postcard perhaps.) I fixed a time when he could visit me at

Bella's flat. I thought I might keep hold of my detachment if we did not meet at the farm.

On the day, at the time I arranged, it was raining; if asked, I would guess it has been raining for most of this month but I am probably wrong. There has been almost no sunshine. I am sure of that. I was watching from Bella's window when the Land Rover arrived and Edward got out. He looked shorter and wider than I expected, seen from above. Then the passenger door opened and Daphne Trigg slid down off the seat and scuttled into the shelter of the porch to the block of flats. I thought at once of your first option, your 'no change' option.

I let them in. In Bella's flat, Daphne looked ordinary and Edward looked awkward. I let them sit down. I let them talk. Edward began. He told me the farmhouse was a sorry place without me, and it was important to him that I came home. Daphne cleared her throat and wriggled her buttocks on the sofa cushions. However, Edward said, I must also realise that I was not the only one who had a right to be considered in whatever arrangements were made. He cared deeply for Daphne, too, and he was not so cruel as to cast her aside now the whole story was out in the open. He hoped that I would recognise Daphne had her own claim to some happiness.

What do you mean? I asked, when he appeared to have run out of platitudes – he went on for longer and used more words and was a lot less clear than I am reporting to you. So it came out, bit by bit, Daphne taking more of the job of explaining it to me as I gave no indication that I was against the whole idea, both of them relaxing, appearing more confident. Edward would buy a house for Daphne to live in, they explained, closer to the farm than she lived now. This would be, as it were, his second home. I would keep my status as a wife, my lovely, big house, lead my life exactly as I had done before, so why should I begrudge her this? Why should I begrudge Edward? We would be behaving like adults, hurting no one.

Was there ever a possibility they would have talked me into this, I wonder? So ready, as I am, to accept that there is another point of view? I hope not. Yet, Edward can be charming, and I had lived with him for so long, it might have been possible I would have softened, pitied him just a little and looked for a way to ease the pain he was in, faced with the disruption of his orderly life. I might have given in because of the instinctive connection between my husband and myself. I stop short of calling it love, though that is the name I have given it and have used to him through the years of our marriage. But he did not come alone, and Daphne was so shallow, so self-seeking in everything she said, and beside her, Edward looked weak, uncertain. I could not even be sure this was a solution he wanted, or if she had manipulated him into requesting it. And of course I am not the woman I was before I started writing to you. I have become clearer to myself as I made myself clear to you. That has given me strength and courage.

They would not go until I had said something in response, so I said I would think about it, which satisfied them – meaningless phrase though it is – and the 'it' left undefined by me but assumed by them to mean the proposition they had laid before me. They were wrong. Instead, I thought through the other options you suggested. But not in the order you suggested them. I thought first about revolution and I understood what you were wanting me to ask myself. Would a room be empty for me, if Edward were not there? The answer to that is not simple, and thinking about it led me back to options two and three. I will tell you why. It has to do with the farm. Would I miss him if he were absent from the farmhouse? Yes.

The rooms in the farmhouse would be crammed with emptiness if Edward were not there. I could scarcely bear to move about the places where he spends his days – the kitchen, where he sits and eats and talks; the snug, a small, untidy, cosy room off the hall where he has his computer and a telephone; the parlour, where he sits with his drink after the day's work. There would be no point to these rooms if Edward were not somewhere close, about to come in, just gone out. But this is true only at the farm. If I were to choose your third option and lay claim to live there alone, making him move elsewhere, he could live wherever he moved to for the rest of his life and, however long that was, when he went at last, the rooms would hold no trace of him. The distinctive smell of a life lived outdoors, among animals and machinery, would soon fade. Once it was gone, no one would look round suddenly in expectation of seeing him, as I expect to see Bella in her flat. Bella's flat is somewhere she lived for a moment. But because she was so vital, so special, so much herself and no one else, she had only to be there for a little while for it to hold a flavour of her in the air when she had gone. The office you describe is not somewhere you saw Birgitt often, not somewhere she visited often, if I understand you correctly, but even if you had never been there before, you could walk into a space she had occupied and feel her loss. I would feel the loss of Edward only in the fabric of the buildings at the place he was born.

I have been conscious, when I have thought of my marriage, which I have done more often lately since starting to write to you, that while I have committed myself to it fully, in every practical sense, I have also held something back. I have kept apart from it in the part of myself where I live when no one and nothing is calling for my attention. I have never stinted in my devotion to Edward, to his physical and emotional needs. I have seen it as my job to do everything possible to make him comfortable and to support him in his work. But I have failed to love the farm, as he loves it. I have felt like a duster moving over its surfaces, keeping it clean. Edward, if he could ever be persuaded to put such fanciful thoughts into words, would see himself as the heart and lungs of the place, keeping it pumping. If he could tell me the truth, he would be forced to admit the farm was more important to him than I am; that he loves me because I am part of the cogs and pistons keeping it going.

Having thought all this, I wondered what it would have been like if Edward had not been a farmer, not been so much obsessed by the place and the job; might I have yielded up my innermost thoughts and feelings and reached a point where every room where he was not was empty? How foolish, you will be saying to yourself; this is like saying, 'If I had married someone else, I might have been happier.' How foolish, I said to myself, as soon as the thought had formed in my mind. It is like saying that his relationship with Daphne Trigg – so much more on the surface than I am, so much clearer in her expressions of joy and sorrow and discontent – is in some way justified by the fact that, while I could reconcile myself to marrying the man, I could not reconcile myself to my place in the hierarchy; subservient to the farm, with all its weight of history and present burden of toil. Nothing justifies what he did; nothing justifies the proposal they put to me. The compromise would have degraded us all.

I watched from the window of Bella's flat as Daphne and Edward left the building. Daphne took a step out from under the porch then stepped back – it was still raining. Edward ran across the car park to the Land Rover and brought it as close as possible to the shelter where Daphne stood. This was a courtesy I would not have expected him to show me. He would have done, I acknowledge, if I had asked. Only I never would have asked. In Daphne's position, I would have accepted that the car was over there, that I was not very far from it and that I had legs. Perhaps Daphne will be better for Edward in some ways than I have been. She will force him to take notice of her.

I understood, during the course of that wet afternoon, how I was necessary to Edward for the purpose of maintaining his comfort; that is, not truly necessary at all. And, not being necessary, I had no reason to stay.

The next day, I drove over to the farm and walked into the kitchen where Daphne and Edward were sitting at the kitchen table, as Edward and I have sat for so many years, drinking tea. They were using, I noticed, my tea cosy. Edward pushed back his chair and stood up, his face flushed, his expression hopeful. Daphne had just lifted a mug to her lips and did not know whether to go ahead and drink out of it, or whether to put it down. In the moment of indecision, she dropped it and it shattered on the stone floor, pieces of it skipping away from the point of impact to lodge in corners and under furniture where I can be sure they will stay for months to come.

'I've come to pack a few things,' I said, and walked on past them.

'You're going?' said Daphne. She sounded hopeful. She had no idea of the burden I was leaving her to shoulder as I left the room.

Edward came after me. In our bedroom, while I began to pack my clothes, he shut the door and told me that, if this was what it took to make me stay, he would stop seeing Daphne. There was no need, he said, to follow the path they had proposed the day before, if I did not like it. We could go back to just the way we were before.

'I'm not going just because of Daphne,' I said. 'I'm going because I don't find the life I am living here, with you, is all I ever want to have.' He sat down on the bed and put his head in his hands. 'The life you led with me isn't everything you wanted, either, was it?' I said. 'If it had been, you would not have turned to Daphne.'

'You're saying it is not all my fault,' he said.

'That is what I'm saying.'

'Will you be coming back?'

'To visit. I have two sons and two grandchildren who live here.'

'Where will you go?'

'I'll let you know when I get there.'

He carried my suitcases down to the car. Daphne was still sitting at the table in a circle of broken mug. I hoisted the tea cosy off the teapot as I passed and tucked it into my bag.

'Oh . . .' she said.

'Knit yourself another,' I said, which was remarkably petty but satisfying.

Edward was still standing watching me go, as I turned the corner of the lane. He has everything that matters most to him left in his life and I honestly believe he will be as happy without me as with me, once he has found someone else to do the chores. It will not, I feel sure, be Daphne.

I have been rereading *The Bog People*, here in my peaty, acid-soiled outpost. I have looked again at the pictures of the Tollund Man's body and read the description of what was best preserved – his heart, lungs, liver; his alimentary canal; his sexual organs; his hat. I have brought my knitted balaclava with me – it is windy here, too, and cold – and I think, as I put it on to go out for a walk, that I am preserved in the same way. Everything vital still in place, but suspended. My skin, like his, is a little the worse for wear; my brain may have shrunk a little. As to my face – Professor Glob describes the Tollund Man's expression as a combination of 'majesty and gentleness'. I wish for this. To be mild but dignified. I look in the mirror and imagine myself into being more like the Tollund Man.

Isn't this where we started?

Raspberries grow well in Scotland, also ferns. It is too early for the raspberry canes to be fruiting, but the ferns will soon begin to unfurl. I know I have decisions still to make, but I need time to contemplate these things before I make them.

Tina

Silkeborg
21st March

Dearest Tina,
I am waiting for you. I will wait, every day, between twelve o'clock and two o'clock in the cafe in the museum. I will be

watching the door, waiting for you to arrive. There is no need to tell me you are coming; though I have never seen your face, I will recognise you. I will know you by the picture you have given me through all these months; a portrait in words. I have listened to everything you have told me and to the silences where I have heard the things you did not say. I hope you will be smiling, as you come through the door, because at last you have reached the place you have always wanted to be. I will be smiling because we will be together. In the same room.

The museum is open every day.

Even if you do not receive this letter, you will know I am waiting. The Tollund Man is waiting too, has been waiting two thousand years for you to come. Please come.

My love, always,

Anders

Author's Note

The Tollund Man is a perfectly preserved body from around 250 BC, unearthed in 1950 in a peat bog in a remote part of Jutland. He has a cap on his head, a belt round his waist and a noose round his neck. Professor P. V. Glob was the Danish archaeologist responsible for the excavation and subsequent study of these remains. He wrote a book, *The Bog People*, which came out in 1969, about this and other finds. In 1970 Seamus Heaney wrote a poem called 'The Tollund Man', which appeared in his collection *Wintering Out* in 1972.

In 2010, Heaney published an essay in *The Times*, revisiting his thoughts about the Tollund Man, before the launch of a new poetry collection, *Human Chain*. At the head of this essay was a photograph of 'the perfectly preserved, mild and meditative face of a neighbour from the Iron Age'. I have had this picture pinned on my wall ever since. Each of the aspects of the Tollund Man that Heaney picks out in this descriptive phrase has haunted me. The remarkable preservation of the body of a man who died two millennia ago, when the bodies of everyone I know who has died in my lifetime are completely lost. The expression of calm thoughtfulness that, even though we know he died by violence, makes it seem he would be a bringer of comfort, if he could only speak. His likeness to men and women alive today, living in the next road, walking down the same street, taking for granted what it would have been the business of his life to strive for – food, safety, warmth. *Meet Me at the Museum* has grown out of my contemplation of the Tollund Man's face.

I have not invented the Silkeborg Museum. It exists, as I have described it, and anyone lucky enough to be in Denmark, who has the time, can visit it. I have invented a person called Anders who I imagine working there. Neither the person nor the job he does is based on any of the people at this gem of a museum or the jobs they do.

Acknowledgements

Thanks to:

James Hawes, for his encouragement, support and advice.

Judith Murray and the team at Greene and Heaton (with special mention for Rose Coyle and Kate Rizzo), and Jane Lawson and the team at Transworld, for being so good at what they do.

Fiona Clarke, Dr Sarah Milliken and Rebecca McKay, for providing early feedback.

Ceri Lloyd, Bev Murray, Elizabeth Crowley, who, with Rebecca McKay, are indispensable writerly friends.

Deborah Warner, for the loan of the inspirational hut.

Anne Youngson worked for many years in senior management in the car industry before embarking on a creative career
as a writer. She has supported many charities in governance
roles, including Chair of the Writers in Prison Network,
which provided residencies in prisons for writers. She lives
in Oxfordshire and is married with two children and three
grandchildren. *Meet Me at the Museum* is her debut novel,
which is due to be published around the world.